Who Wrote the Book of Love?

Who Wrote the Book of Love?

Thomas Farber

Donald S. Ellis, Publisher, San Francisco
Creative Arts Book Company
1984

All the characters in these stories, including the narrative "I," are no more or less than fictions: they represent no actual people, living or dead. Though for me these characters speak to life as I know it—and now seem real to me, so much time have I spent with them—they in fact inhabit only the domain of my imagination. THOMAS FARBER

For information contact: Creative Arts Book Company, 833 Bancroft Way, Berkeley, California 94710.

Grateful acknowledgement is made to Gold Hill Music, Inc., for permission to quote the lines from "Love the One You're With," by Stephen Stills, on page 10.

Copyright © 1977 by Thomas Farber
Printed in the United States of America
All Rights Reserved

ISBN: 0-916870-69-3
Library of Congress Catalog Card No. 84-045096

For my parents

Who Wrote the Book of Love?

The good singers of old time, Béroul and Thomas of Built, Gilbert and Gottfried told this tale for lovers and none other, and, by my pen, they beg you for your prayers. They greet those who are cast down, and those in heart, those troubled and those filled with desire, those who are overjoyed and those disconsolate, all lovers. May all herein find strength against inconstancy, against unfairness and despite and loss and pain and all the bitterness of loving.

JOSEPH BEDIER
The Romance of Tristan and Iseult

Down at the Bay early that morning, southwest wind strong in his face, he passed a long hour watching the boats beat out toward the Gate. Cold and cleansed, he was on his way to work, moving slowly with the weekday traffic, when he spotted Ellen walking out of a market. Pulling up to the curb, he honked to get her attention, and she came over to the car. He hadn't seen her for more than a year, and had never really known her well. She and a friend of his had tried living together but separated after several months.

As she sat in the car, she did most of the talking, speaking intensely about her new career. "I like being a nurse," she told him. "I've always wanted to help people. But I've found, as I could have predicted, that most of their pain is beyond care. There are things I can do, of course, and I'm glad to know what I've learned, but the evidence of my senses only confirms what I've always believed: people suffer. Pleasure turns out just to be a brief deviation from the way things really are."

He felt tempted to laugh at her tragic view. There they were, in fine health, sun shining, wind strong enough to wash away all sorrows. It seemed an unnecessary act of will to insist there could be anything not consonant with the day itself. But he didn't laugh. Something in her tone, past the words themselves, summoned up despair, heartbreak, loneliness, loss. She was, he conceded to himself, speaking of what was also real.

As she talked, her incredibly thin and long lips occasionally curled into a tight smile, especially when she confirmed yet another bleak conclusion. "You know, people take years to die. After a while no one comes to visit. They can't do anything themselves. They can't

Who Wrote the Book of Love?

even find the strength to give up." She looked at him hard, daring him to refute her point.

Her pessimism reminded him of the '50s, when it had been so much the fashion to identify with madness and isolation. But as she spoke, her enormous blue eyes taking him in, unblinking, he had no desire to mock. She was too beautiful.

"I have to get back to the hospital now," she said, checking her watch. "I'm in the phone book. Call me sometime. We all need people." She smiled, gathered her packages, and was gone.

Driving to his office, he grinned to himself at her seriousness, and wondered what she'd be like—with him—if she weren't bound to such severe truths. But there really was no point thinking about it. She regarded happiness as merely illusory, after all; any pleasures they shared would only make her uneasy. He wouldn't be able to win for losing. Even worse, however much she gainsaid her nursing career, her affection was clearly reserved for those most in need. Not ill, not broken, without enemies, needing no more than someone to love, he wouldn't have a chance with her. Again grinning to himself, he wondered if anyone had ever told her that a man can die of a broken heart.

Approaching his office, he dismissed the notion of asking her out. Finding the right person was hard enough without trying to argue someone into having a good time. Turning up the radio, he was pleased to hear his favorite tune, and sang along:

> Well, there's a rose in the fisted glove
> and the eagle flies with the dove,
> and if you can't be with the one you love, honey,
> love the one you're with, love the one you're with . . .

When he returned to his apartment that evening, it was nearly nightfall. Just as he entered, picking up the cat, turning on the lights, the phone rang. It was his brother calling long distance. "Listen," his brother said. "I have very bad news. Daddy is dead."

Hours later these were the words still in his ears, but long since he was saying them to himself, crying. After a while, walking from room to room still saying the words, he began to prepare to head home in the morning. He made a plane reservation, arranged to have his neighbors care for the cat, and spoke briefly to close friends to tell them what had happened. When they offered to come by, he asked them not to. He said he didn't know just how long he'd be gone.

Alone in the apartment, packed and ready to go, dazed, he wondered what to do until morning. Pacing, unable to settle, he looked up Ellen's number and dialed. When she answered he apologized for calling so late and then, finding no better words, said:

"My dad just died."

"Why don't you come over?" she replied.

Her apartment was small, spartan, and not very clean. It wasn't what he needed, he thought, as he walked in. And it was just too foreign, anyway. Of course she had no idea who his father had been, what their family was like, where he came from. He had made a mistake in calling, a mistake in coming over. This was no time for strangers.

She returned from the kitchen with a glass and a decanter of wine. "Drink," she said. He drank. And kept drinking.

"My dad's dead," he said after a while. "I don't usually drink much, and then not wine." He drank some more. "Do you think it's wrong to be getting drunk when your dad has died?" he asked her. She kept filling the glass.

"I have to be at the airport at nine," he said, absently, when the decanter was half empty.

"I'll set the alarm," she replied.

When the wine was finished, she guided him to the bed and helped him undress. Then she undressed and joined him under the covers.

"My dad died," he was saying. "Now my dad is dead."

She smiled a long, thin smile and took him in her arms. As they came close to each other he tried, through the alcohol, to ask himself if this was right. His dad had died, and here he was going to make

Who Wrote the Book of Love?

love. Closing his eyes, he could see his father at the kitchen table, exhausted after a long day's work, soon losing the drift of the family's mealtime chatter, clenching and unclenching his fingers, staring at them as if still amazed that they could have lost their strength.

But then, coming back from so far away, he was in her, and could see her eyes staring up at him, enormous, blue, unblinking.

 Within days of their first meeting both felt they were playing for enormous stakes. The very pleasure they found in each other created anxiety: was it "real"; could it be sustained; was there good faith? Relationships in flux all around them, the motives of others always mysterious, each imagined countless possible impediments. He took a first step, canceling a long planned extended vacation. She was very glad he wasn't going, but didn't know just what had changed his mind. He didn't explain, and she decided it was too forward to ask. A week later, feeling overwhelmed, she went away for several days. He was devastated. There was no way for him to know how much she missed him. Or, rather, she told him so on her return, but he wasn't sure her words meant all he hoped they did.

Continuing to see each other, feeling elated but utterly exposed, they tried with questions to paint in the unknown terrain, as if the answers might somehow lessen the risk.

"Why did you quit school?"

"Do you like living alone?"

"Have you been in love many times?"

"Why did you two separate?"

And, late at night, when pleasure only heightened the understanding of how costly loss would be: "Who *are* you?"

One afternoon they went up to the park on the rim of the hills. Putting down their packs, they began what proved to be a long game of hide-and-seek, the chase and evasion increasingly intense as minutes passed. Successfully concealing herself behind a boulder, she waited till he passed and then shadowed him as he searched, barely muffling her laughter. But then she lost sight of him. He had sensed her presence, and, doubling back around behind her, suddenly came

Who Wrote the Book of Love?

running, whooping as he closed the distance. Cornered, she picked up a branch. When he charged and wrestled her down, she fought back, flailing her legs, trying to bite his hands as he strained to pin her shoulders. Finally, exhausted, she bared her gums and hissed.

He rolled away. "I give up," he said, laughing. "No more, please, no more."

"Time out," she said. After all, it was only a game. Still, lying on their backs, they kept their distance from each other for a while.

Later, stoned, watching the sun sink in the sky, they spotted some hikers far below.

"Wouldn't it be fine to have some chocolate?" she said. "I bet those people have some."

"One of us should go find out," he replied.

"But which one?"

"Let's throw fingers to see," he said.

Because she didn't know what throwing fingers was, he explained that one of them would take "odds," the other "evens." They'd then count "once, twice, three, *shoot,*" each throwing one or two fingers on the word "shoot." The total number of fingers would be odd or even; one of them would win.

"But no flinching," he added.

"What's flinching?"

"Hesitating to see what your opponent does before committing yourself."

"Cheating?"

"That's it," he replied.

Studying each other's faces, second-and then third-guessing each other, finally they made their choices. She grimaced when she read the count.

"Head on down," he said, laughing.

She thought it over for a moment, and then said: "This is ridiculous. They won't have any chocolate anyway. And besides, they're almost gone. It's too far."

"None of that matters," he replied. "You lost. You have to go."

"I don't *have* to do anything," she said, watching the hikers disappear out of view.

He was angry, but kept himself in check. They had made a bargain, he felt, and she was violating it. For the moment the game seemed a metaphor of all exchange between them. Without trust what was there? Further, he resented the way she had escalated the argument, implying that he was forcing her to go for the chocolate. Though he acknowledged to himself that he might have chosen his words more carefully, still he felt she was being capricious.

"You welshed," he finally said.

"What's welshing?"

"Backing out of a bet when you lose."

"It's your game, not mine," she replied.

They sat silent as the sun dropped behind the mountains on the far side of the Bay. "Time for us to go," he said curtly. She gave him a long look and then headed down toward the car.

In the months that followed they went abroad. Given the inevitable strains of travel, each worked to be as fair as possible to the other. Nor was this onerous, both repeatedly amazed at how quickly bad feeling passed, how their bond seemed of itself to be renewed each morning.

It was perhaps not strange that throwing fingers became part of their relationship. Instead of arguing about who would wash the dishes or fetch the laundry, they generally let the game settle the question. Trying to predict the other's strategy, thinking back to the previous time or the time before that, often hysterical with anticipation, they played over and again. Occasionally, hoping for reprieve, the loser would propose "two out of three." Though the winner of course had no obligation to continue, there was on the other hand the lure of a more decisive victory. Only rarely did they play three out of five. And always without question now, both honored the outcome.

After they had been together for more than a year, they crossed some invisible line of trust. Due to more than familiarity, the trust was warranted because each avoided compromising the other, offering

Who Wrote the Book of Love?

apologies before conflicts went too far, for instance, or not making disagreements public. Though both were strong-willed, they collaborated on not being unreasonable.

One night they lay in bed together, both tired.

"Do you want to make love?" she asked him.

"I don't know," he said, "I'm pretty wiped. But maybe."

"Let's throw fingers," she said. They did, and he lost. Lying beside her, he didn't immediately move. Since an impartial mediator would surely have granted him a moment or two, this wasn't yet a violation of the rules of the game. But several minutes passed and still he lay on his back. Raising herself on her elbow, she looked down into his eyes. He returned her look. Clearly the stares contained an element of challenge, but she had no wish to force a confrontation. She lay down again. Both looked up at the ceiling.

"Well," she finally said. "Are you going to just lie there?"

She was being more than fair, he admitted to himself. She could have said something sharper, or remained silent, retaining the threat of all she might say. Certainly she was going out of her way to be conciliatory. She was making it easy for him, but he was surprised to find that, still, he wasn't moving. Though this was just the kind of minor betrayal he believed undercut the possibility of larger trust, he found himself on the verge of playing it out. Perhaps he'd provoke her to leave the bed. Then in the morning he'd come up with some lame explanation, or stomp out of the house, or insist hotly that it wasn't important. In any of these ways furthering his breach of faith.

Thinking all this, he had a moment of panic. Could it happen on even less than a whim, could it be so almost inadvertent?

Throwing off the covers, he was relieved to find himself sitting up. He was that far, anyway. He took a deep breath, exhaled slowly. Closed his eyes, opened them, surveyed the room. Everything in its place? Ceiling above, floor below, bureau against the wall. Ah, well, he was himself again. He stretched, yawned, looked down at her. And then, reaching to embrace her, a kiss on his lips, he said:

"It's me; I'm here; here I am."

 They sit in her living room, the day waning. Pauline's an old friend and, in these hard times, a friend indeed. Someone to talk to, someone who'll understand, someone who knows them both. Solace, advice, affirmation, affection without demand, that's what he needs. Help.

Pauline makes herself comfortable in the soft chair, opens a fresh pack of cigarettes, lays several down before her in a neat row on the table. She pours a glass of wine, draws the bowl of crackers closer.

"You know," she says, looking at him across the darkening room, "you two should really have separated years ago."

"Why is that?" he says quickly, skin too thin to check his response, nearly any remark about their relationship promising new hurt, new guilt.

"Well," Pauline replies, drawing on her cigarette, laying it down carefully in the ashtray, "you and Dale really wanted different things."

Really wanted different things. He hears the words and tries to bring them to bear on the time they lived together. Of course they'd finished by wanting different things, but that was when they were separating. The words suggest a handle but don't really deliver any understanding of where and how the separation began. Weighing the phrase, irritated that it offers no saving formula, he is at the same time relieved to discover no new area of remorse.

"Not only that," Pauline goes on, "but Dale was too young for you." *Too young for you.* Is that it? But he was also young when they met, they met as equals, he'd been lucky to find her, everyone envied them. And, Jesus Christ, no older women were going around offering themselves to him.

Who Wrote the Book of Love?

Or were they? A year before he met Dale, he and Pauline spent a few nights together. But that was different, his heart never opened to her. Pauline had seemed to feel the same. Or had she?

The question takes him to dangerous ground and he backs off. He needs to work it through, needs friends. Pauline understands. She's been kind. She knows them both.

"She told me we never really knew each other," he says.

Pauline laughs. "You don't have to worry that one. People are always telling each other that kind of thing when they separate. It sounds much worse than it is."

"That's probably true," he says. "I'm trying not to read what we had between us in terms of the present. And I try not to listen when she does. I think I know her. I'm pretty sure we knew each other. We had something good together." He makes these last three assertions without much conviction, and looks to Pauline, hoping she'll nod.

"Of course," Pauline says, meeting his eyes, "everyone is capable of change."

Capable of change. The words sound fair enough. But capable of this change? Whatever had been between them, even the difficulties he initiated, he'd presumed that they were together. All disagreements —from each to other—had seemed to him to move out from that sure center. *Capable of change* barely hinted at the violence he felt in their separation.

"Anyway," Pauline continues, "the way it looks to me, she'll just play the two of you off, one against the other, as long as she can."

This he can't agree to, but Pauline isn't at fault, she doesn't know all the facts. There's much he hasn't told her. When Dale left him, she said she was sorry but she was following her heart. *Following her heart.* Who could argue with that? Could he tell Pauline he had used every cheap trick in the book to badger Dale into seeing him occasionally, that he had implored her, finally with success, to be unfaithful to her new lover? It was perhaps true that Dale now wouldn't mind having him on a string. But surely she hadn't set up the terms of the game, not by herself, anyway.

What Pauline might tell him, what he might learn, then, is limited by how much of the truth he can stand to reveal.

"I wouldn't put it past her," Pauline adds.

And what Pauline can give him is limited also by what he'll allow her to say. He has no use for sharp words against Dale. Still she is primary in his life. These people he now talks to so much, needs so much, who are they? They were and are friends. No more, if no less. But what he had with her was beyond his feeling for all others. Now, in simply talking about her, these others seem to him to move toward occupying her space in his life. Imposing with even the most neutral words on what for him is still hers, between them, committed. He has in no way given her up, though everything his friends say to him presumes that she is gone.

"Did you hear me?" Pauline asks.

But he hasn't heard, he's somewhere else, working to remember a poem he once had to learn in school. Slowly he finds the lines:

> . . . Love is not love
> Which alters when it alteration finds,
> Or bends with the remover to remove.

 An old and very wealthy man, mane of white hair down to his shoulders, liberal for his ilk, though for him Franklin Roosevelt will always be the man who betrayed his own class. "Rosenfeld," he calls him.

A lifelong celibate, the old man has not been without feelings of affection, particularly for young men of promise. When he dies, his Georgian mansion, Episcopal chapel, art collection, and King Charles spaniels will go to Yale. "They call it a 'meritocracy' now," he snorts. "Technocrats!"

He sits with cigar and brandy in the living room, servant clearing away the dishes. "I never felt free to take a lover until my mother died," he says, smiling wryly, "and by then I was well past fifty. At that point in my life it seemed a little late for beginnings." He guillotines the tip of his cigar, strikes a match. "As you might imagine, my mother was a woman of considerable force."

Often snide when speaking of those seeking the power he was born with, still he understands that nothing remains the same. "Shirtsleeves to shirtsleeves in three generations," he remarks, talking about the profligate and now impecunious grandson of a turn-of-the-century Brahmin financier. Though his people have matriculated at Yale for two hundred years, he is perhaps intentionally the last of his line, aware nonetheless that wealth has afforded him freedom, calm, and scruples others might do well to possess. Without pretending to feel the passions of the recipients, he's donated freely to many causes, some well to the left of center. And over the years each new wave of civic leaders has been invited out to visit, less to advance any selfish interest of his than to show them a way of life possibly worth preserving, if only for someone—one of them?—hungry enough to reach for it.

"Money makes power," he says, laughing, and recounts the story of one of the countless requests for support he's received. "Do you know the rest? Yes. Power corrupts." He laughs again.

His secretary, a single woman of sixty, comes in with a message before scurrying out. Obsequious in his presence, she tyrannizes anyone trying to reach him, demanding for herself all the deference his name commands. "Her thirtieth year with me," he says, watching as she closes the door. "We were made for each other, apparently. I have it, she needs it. Came from nothing, poor woman. Raised in a basement apartment. A curious person," he adds, as if finding her hungers inevitable but still well beyond actual comprehension. Something in his tone suggests that he's made a decision not to understand her feelings, as though—for all his good works—it would be absurd, or, worse, disloyal to his inheritance, to forgo the distance and coolness he was bred to.

Out the window of his private library the estate stretches for thousands of acres, hedgerows carefully tended, sheep grazing, river winding by, punt at the dock. Over the cooing of his doves the roar of a rush hour miles away is carried down by the breeze. On a table by his writing desk, beside several books by Thomas Merton, lies a finely printed edition, beautifully bound, of the poems of Sappho.

 One day, late in the afternoon, she came up the stairs past the yellow blood roses to the porch where he was sitting in the sun. Down in the yard Al hammered on an engine.

"Hello," she said with a noticeable accent. "My name is Rita. Your sister gave me your address. She said to ask you if I could stay here when I passed through. We have mutual friends in New York City. I'll be here five days on vacation before I fly home to teach in Vienna."

"Sure," he said, "you can stay. There's plenty of room, see for yourself." They went inside the apartment, and he gave her the large back bedroom. Though clean, it was empty except for a dresser, lamp, and mattress on the floor.

"No one in this place but me," he said. "Not too much furniture either. But it's home. I camp up front in the little room by the porch. Right under the plum tree. Make yourself comfortable. Stay as long as you like. You won't bother me."

He made some sandwiches and, while they ate at the kitchen table, she spoke of the many places she had visited around the country. She showed him photos, too, most of the Southwest. He took his guitar out and was still playing when she went to settle down in her room.

An hour later he stopped by her door, knocked, and gave her some towels and a key to the house. Telling her to take anything in the refrigerator if she was hungry, he said he was going out.

When he returned late that evening, he saw her door ajar, the light still on. He sat in the kitchen for a few minutes playing the guitar, then put it away. Checking the front door, he washed up and got into bed.

Just as he was dozing off several minutes later, she appeared at the threshold of his room. Standing there, wearing a nightgown, she said: "Do you mind if I come in?"

"If you like," he replied.

She walked over to his bed and slipped in under the covers.

The next morning he was up early making coffee when she emerged from his room.

"Morning," he said.

"Good morning."

They sat in silence at the kitchen table, until finally she asked: "Where did you go last night?"

"To a party."

"You didn't think to invite me?"

"No."

"Why?"

"I wanted to go alone."

She smiled a weak smile and then, after another silence, asked: "Do women often come to your house like that and sleep with you?"

"I can't say it's a regular thing," he answered.

"Are you glad I came into your room?"

"I enjoyed making love with you."

"Do you like me?"

"I don't know you yet," he said.

Later that day they drove up into the dry autumn hills where they could see the sweep of the Bay below. Down at the harbor later, they walked out to the end of the long pier, watched the shark fishermen, got cold, and returned to the apartment. That night they made love again.

Life in the apartment the next three days was quiet. Each morning after coffee he sat in the kitchen playing the guitar. The phone rang, friends dropped by, he went out on errands. Late each afternoon he showed her other parts of the town, quietly describing the history, animal life, climate, and terrain. Each evening they watched the sun set behind the mountains at the far side of the Bay. And then each

Who Wrote the Book of Love?

night, soon after dinner, she came into his room.

In the kitchen the morning she was to go she said: "You know, I think I'm in love with you." He said nothing in reply. "But, sadly," she then continued, "I have to go. School begins in a week." Still he was silent. She looked over at the clock. "I think we should leave now," she said. As they went down the stairs she took one of the yellow blood roses.

At the airport they had coffee in silence. When they reached the final check-in area she stood holding the rose, clearly hoping he would respond to what she had said. He looked at her carefully, trying to imagine how far away she would soon be, from how far away she had come. Wondering what she had to believe was between them. For him she had simply come out of thin air up the stairs, Al hammering on the engine below. She had stayed five days; they had shared some pleasures. And now, into thin air once more, she was leaving.

But seeing her standing there holding the rose, he decided to try. "Turn around," he said. She did. Then he whispered in her ear: "When you turn around again, I'll be gone." And he was.

When she moved out, she packed up not only what she had brought to the apartment when they first decided to live together but also what she had acquired since. Quilts, rugs, pans, clothes, lamps, wicker baskets, paints, sheets, the stereo. Her things.

She also took those artifacts which, though "theirs," both tacitly agreed were more hers than his. Some birds' nests, an old lute, most of the records. There was no quarrel over her choices. Finally out of words, he simply watched her, dizzied by the efficiency and apparent finality of her departure. She seemed in a very great hurry to begin her new life.

Alone in the apartment when she was gone, measuring what remained, his eye caught a hook on the wall. A woodcut had hung there, no larger than four by six inches, black and white. A bare tree with gnarled roots on a cliff just over the ocean; clouds edging past a moon setting into a too-close horizon; oversized stars sweeping through the branches down to the sea.

The picture had been a gift. Four years before, in Athens, they had been dinner guests at the family home of one of his old college friends. That night they learned that his friend's father, a surveyor, was also an artist. Completely unschooled, he had been painting for years. Blanketing the walls was an extraordinary sequence of watercolors of the planets, brilliant vistas of their surfaces as the painter imagined them, naive and exuberant.

She had laughed with pleasure at the watercolors, repeatedly praising them. Later that evening his friend's father had given them the woodcut. At home they mounted it on the hook on the wall.

If, less taken than she with the visual arts, he had not fully shared her immediate delight with the paintings, if her enthusiasm was the probable proximate cause of the gift, the woodcut had nonetheless been given to *them*. Seeing it on the wall each day, he had come to treasure it and, through it, his memory of that evening.

As he thought about the woodcut, he was struck with the thought that it was not only these objects she had taken that were gone. Rather, because she was the only other witness to their time together, because without her there was so much he would not remember, that would have no further resonance, her departure threatened to cut him off from what they had lived between them.

This thought then crystallized in his mind, that she was the key to the door of his recollection of their shared past. Without her it was lost. And apart from the issue of their separation, he didn't want to lose those years, that life.

Because she had no wish to see him in the months that followed, he found himself looking for her on the street, at the market, in bookstores, at films. Occasionally bumping into her, reaffirming her sheer physical reality, he was able to renew his hold on the life they had shared. More often than not, however, he had to settle for glimpses of her as she drove by in her car.

The next year he lost track of her completely. Unable to find any listing for her in the phone book, desolate, he thought perhaps she had left town. It now often seemed to him that what they had experienced between them simply had never been. Whole sections—vital sections —of his life were disappearing.

Then one day, coming home from work, he saw her getting out from behind the wheel of a different car. He grinned with pleasure. Contact had been reestablished. Once more he felt he had access to his memory. She was still real. He could touch the fabric of what they had shared.

Soon after, things improved even more. Apparently she had moved into his neighborhood, for he saw the car parked nearby each day. Try as he would, however, he couldn't match her schedule. Despite daily passes up and down the street, he never saw her.

As time passed he continued to look for her, but the door on what they had lived between them was shutting tight. He could now remember only the shadows of their shared past, as though it had been inhabited by others, if at all.

It was in this way, still more time passing, that when he tried to picture her, and so what they had experienced together, he could summon up no more than an image of the car.

 This was a case of the child saving the parent. Several years before, the son not yet even a twinkle in his father's eye, the revolution had clearly been imminent, palpable if nonetheless just out of reach. Regulars on the block lived for, banked on, cataclysmic transformation. And then, just like that, almost faster than it had appeared, the wave of the apocalypse receded, leaving them high and dry. Like other regulars, Larry continued to stop by the cafés to take in the changes, he still hung out on the block to see what the street people were into, but it was over. Not only could the remaining fragments not re-create the whole, but, memory all too fallible, it was impossible to hold on to the feeling of collective power that had inspired them. So it was that the junkies, whose stylized suicide had only recently seemed both needlessly pessimistic and inexcusably private, now warranted another look. At least their days had an accessible pattern. They had a handle, if only the handle on death's door.

Nowhere to go, Larry took to living in his car, though like everything which looked more or less the same as before, this was now no freedom. He felt more like a wino than a revolutionary, slept in vacant lots, walked the streets bouncing a rubber ball. He applied for Aid to the Totally Disabled not as a shuck for easy money but because he was desperate. What was the job market for former revolutionaries? If he once wondered what would happen when the Thermidorian reaction set in—governments seldom cherish anarchists, he'd often joked—at least then his life would have had a context, recognition, if only negative. But now, alone, he could barely connect his present to any past, least of all a heroic one. Nothing to do, he pored over the daily paper, averting his eyes from stories about suicides off the Golden Gate Bridge.

Then he met Sarah. While she herself felt shaky, having only recently won independence from her husband and his academic routine, she at least had the house from the divorce settlement. Larry soon moved in, and though he was often despondent, she valued him for being all her husband was not. Beyond the system, an outlaw, this even as he steadily berated himself for having wasted his life. If only he hadn't quit accounting school, he kept saying.

At his urging they sold the house and moved to the country. A new life, though the past followed them in the form of Sarah's ex-husband. Crazed since the day she left him, he plastered the rural community with flyers accusing Larry of woman-stealing. In spite of him, however, things quickly settled into place. Soon, at Larry's request, Sarah stopped using contraceptives. And then Glen was born.

Larry was elated. He wanted not only Sarah and Glen but all they implied. A wife and child to build his life around, to warrant and necessitate an entire range of commitments. He felt strange to have to be so intentional about what most people simply did, he knew there must be some middle ground, but for the moment it eluded him. He needed structure badly, could barely imagine how he'd once felt secure enough to mock all he now sought. He could occasionally remember the confidence of the recent past, but found no way to bring it to bear on the present.

Breadwinner of his family—and grateful to have the role—he attended night school at a local junior college and passed the real estate exam. Former compatriots on the block couldn't believe it, accused him of selling out. What could be more capitalist than a middleman in property exchanges? Could Larry have forgotten that "the land belongs to no one"? No, he hadn't forgotten, but he had to make a living. Had to support his wife and child. Yearned to support them lest he disintegrate completely. Jobs were scarce for the "unskilled." Real estate was at least open to anyone willing to work on commission. And while political rhetoric had once come easily to his lips, he'd never been an ideologue. The Vietnam war, the class war, racism, these had been real to him primarily as they referred back to

Who Wrote the Book of Love?

the camaraderie of people working together, dreaming together, to make social change. If he had lacked the clarity and dedication of others in the vanguard, he was, on the other hand, not so different from "the people."

Working long hours, he began to earn good money. Throwing in his commission toward the down payment, he bought a home. Then, taking a second mortgage, he purchased a beach house, renting it out to build equity. He drove clients around in a new car, marveling at how easy it was to get credit. "All you have to do is play the game," he kept saying in wonder. When things were tough—commissions sometimes came few and far between; he pushed himself too hard; and clients often assumed he was their adversary—he'd think of going back on Aid to the Totally Disabled. But Sarah and Glen needed him. He kept at it. He dreamed of accumulating property, giving Glen a Frank Lloyd Wright for his twenty-first birthday. Maybe two Frank Lloyd Wrights.

Despite the pressures of work he loved spending time with his son, watching him by degrees interact with and master the world around him. "Glen keeps me sane," he often said, laughing, changing a dirty diaper. And Glen kept growing, by age two strong and hot-tempered. Willful little fucker! Denied something, he'd give one angry look of warning, and, no concession forthcoming, would pee on the floor to get even. But nothing could dismay Larry: Glen was his reason for living.

In this period Sarah decided to move out and live by herself. Not that she loved him less, she told Larry, but she just had to give it a try or she'd always feel too dependent on him. There was little argument. Though an integral component of the life Larry had chosen so intentionally was being removed, Sarah was clearly speaking of a real need. How could he fight it? They found her an apartment, saw each other often and amicably, and shared care of the child.

Spending long hours with Glen, always confirmed and comforted by his sheer existence, Larry was repeatedly impressed by his son's straightforward—and undeniable—wants. Stoned, he'd watch Glen run naked around the living room, small penis bobbing up and down. No doubt about it, he often thought, Glen was a miniature adult. "Come here, little man," he'd call, laughing. Little man. And so it went, night after night, month after month, watching, learning, until Larry, whose understanding had once been couched in the language of revolution, now viewed life as far more elemental. Shit, piss, hunger, love, this is what he saw.

Time passing, he gave more and more consideration to these basic urges which, he was sure, underpinned all social action. Selling a home, sneaking hits off a joint, he'd stand back and observe a couple as they argued about whether to take it, viewing them not as husband and wife but as two overgrown children. He could appreciate their needs, wasn't putting them down, but he just couldn't see them as they saw themselves. As for himself, he had ever less desire to clothe his own hungers in finery. "I'm just a little doggie," he'd say, laughing. "Any woman who loves me has to understand that. Watching me pee on some tree, sniffing someone's tail. Seeing it's no big deal. Just ol' Larry doin' his thing."

Spending time at a singles bar, initially hoping to replace Sarah, in time he came to enjoy just finding someone for the night. No pretenses, no promises. He wasn't averse to having things work out with Sarah, or anyone else for that matter, but it didn't have to happen. Or, if it did, he didn't have to confuse commitment with his simple needs. "Pussy!" he'd shout, walking around the house half naked. "Gonna get some pussy tonight!"

As Glen continued to grow, the rural community boomed and began to suffer certain urban ailments. A pistol-carrying prowler terrorized the town with a series of rape/burglaries. Appointed block captain for the citizen's patrol, Larry walked around at night with a flashlight and police whistle on the lookout for a black man wearing a yellow cap.

Not surprisingly, while on patrol he came to know his neighbors better. Now they of course had good reason to talk to him; seeing him as their defender, they became more open. It was in this way that he

Who Wrote the Book of Love?

found he didn't have to go to the singles bar to meet someone to spend the night with. "You understand," he said, talking about the rapist, "in this day and age no one is worried about fucking *per se*. It's just a question of who does it, and on what terms." Savoring the irony, that being on rape patrol led him into so many beds, he had to laugh. It made complete sense to him, son Glen his guru, that under any sky he would always find the earth.

 I was back in town for the summer wedding of a good friend. Relatives from both families stood under the elm, smiling at their in-laws-to-be, waiting for the music to begin.

Clearly pleased with the occasion, they were nonetheless surprised to find themselves under the canopy of the tree. Still, if having the ceremony outdoors was the greatest shock they were to receive from the young people—this in a time of couples living together without benefit of clergy—then so be it. It was, after all, a wedding.

How people point to the future, how they turn from the past! Surely the adults gathered there knew that the bride's parents had woven between them a web of intricate misery. That her mother, suddenly stricken with new symptoms of a long suffered neurosis, had asked the couple to postpone the wedding until she was healed. That, no delay forthcoming—her daughter was reaching for a star—the symptoms miraculously disappeared in time for the mother, too, to be present under the elm.

And surely the adults standing there knew the story of the groom's parents, how his mother moved to a remote town to share the life of her relentlessly pragmatic husband. How after ten years and two sons in that dreamless union she had taken her life.

But this day the past was to defer to the future. Beams of light worked down through thick leaves to the friends and relatives waiting below. Then, before any wicked witch could curse the match, guitar and flute struck up Vivaldi, and they were walking toward us across the green. Simple white brocade for her, a peasant shirt for him. Hand in hand.

The ceremony was brief, another blessing. When the glass broke

Who Wrote the Book of Love?

under his shoe, her eyes had a wild look of triumph.

I was moved. Perhaps these traditional forms could carry them through the perils of the here and now. Perhaps the love they promised would endure. I wanted to believe that the clarity of their public statement would sustain them.

The marriage made, we all began to move back across the green for refreshments. I fell into step beside the groom's father. Since his wife's suicide nearly twenty years before, he had remained a bachelor. A successful small businessman, phenomenally uninterested in anything beyond his immediate circle, he played golf and bridge, had occasional girl friends, and lived a life of easy routine.

"Well," he said to me, "you're his friend, what did you think?"

"A time for celebration, C. G.," I responded. "They looked wonderful."

"And what about yourself, anyway" he said. "A fella your age ought to be thinking about doing the same as my boy."

"But no one's asked me yet, C. G.," I replied, grinning.

"You'd best not wait for that," he said, without a smile. "You're not getting any younger."

In his blunt way, unfortunately, C. G. had given voice to Truth. I wasn't getting any younger, and just then I was feeling my age. And of course the wedding left me sentimental for the fresh start I wasn't making, for the words of promise that weren't on my lips. It wouldn't take much of this kind of talk to make me blue.

"Someone your age ought to settle down, get married, raise a family," C. G. went on. "This is what a man needs."

"But why is that, C. G.?" I asked. "You seem to be doing pretty well on your own."

By now we had arrived at the bar and were both reaching for our drinks.

"I am doing pretty well," he said, "but that's different. Very different. You see, I've been through it. I know. I've got my boys. You need family, yes, you need family. Someone to bury you."

 Competitive, acerbic, and overweight, earning an almost-six-figure salary diminished somewhat by alimony payments to his first wife, he climbs heavily out of his BMW after a long day at the office. Coming inside the house, calling "Anybody home?," he walks back to the bedroom and lies down to watch Monday Night Football. Her husband.

Though now, after two years of marriage, much of what he is and does repels her, his second wife can make no claim that he misrepresented himself to her. That is to say, while courting her he never performed stoned late-night Charlie Chaplin routines, intimating some secret self only she could release. And, no Othello, he never wooed her with the hardships he had endured. Truth be told, he did little more than act naturally to win her, since she was prepared to love him—or someone like him—well before they met. Like us all, she respected power, and was to some degree influenced by the opinions of those around her. Working in state government just after college, she could hardly remain unaware of the admiration he inspired in the bureaucratic world. In no time at all she saw him as others did.

Though no Adonis, he was decisive, confident of his acumen, and could defend even questionable decisions with real conviction. Nor in his meteoric rise as a technocrat did it discomfit him to dominate men of less power, intelligence, or certitude. Elected officials particularly were impressed by the brisk way he could list "the options."

When he met his second wife, she was committed to social change but pragmatic enough to try working within the system, bright, quick with words, and very good-looking. It would perhaps be unfair to suggest that he wanted her as a showpiece, but he seemed not to perceive that those qualities in her it gave him status to possess might also contain an essence capable of repudiating his own. Or perhaps he intuited that, already in politics, she'd be willing to let appearances stand for reality so long as others were impressed. Whichever, he bought the BMW to show her that he too was a free spirit, and proposed. Several important people attended their wedding.

Early in the marriage she had misgivings about certain things her husband did, small things, to be sure, probably not even worth thinking about. His behavior at parties, for instance. There was something disconcerting about the way he'd stand clapping his hands to the beat while she did the latest step with some black man wearing platform shoes and a shirt split down to the navel. She admired her husband for not trying to be hip, was always flattered when he told her she was the best dancer on the floor. Yet particularly since he never seemed in the least bit jealous of her partners, she occasionally had the unsettling feeling that he found it too easy to say he couldn't dance, as if suggesting that such matters—the physical, the sexual?—were secondary to the real stuff of his life. But then, dancing by him, seeing his rumpled slacks and scuffed shoes, she'd again be charmed by his unfashionableness. He was what he was.

She was more troubled by the amount of traveling he did. He was always flying off to some conference for a day, often crossing the country and returning the same night. At first this had some allure: place names beckoned and the miles looked like freedom. But then they went abroad to three countries in five days. Though she met several cabinet-level ministers and their wives, she came home unconvinced that it made any sense. They had been exhausted from jet lag, the conferences on higher education were held in airport hotels, and this was just the moment when everyone was talking at cocktail parties about the fuel crisis and how to live more ecologically. Worst of all, her husband had put her on his payroll to write a memo on the meeting, but, going through her pages of notes, she could find little of value to report.

Soon after this trip she stopped working as a legislative aide, returning to painting and her old friends, though most of what entertaining she and her husband did together was for his colleagues. Back at a craft and spending time with people who lived more quietly, she was glad to be out of politics. If already she wished her husband had a different kind of work, she felt only more affection for him thinking of the price he paid. All those backbiting politicians and administrators, all that travel. Often he'd come home exhausted and fall asleep within minutes. But she loved him all the more; she rued the toll his job was taking.

Things began to change when they made a long deferred trip to the mountains to visit some of her friends who were eking out a living as farmers. There her husband's verbal skill suddenly seemed only aggressive, and she found herself both admiring what her friends had created and wanting to explain or, even, apologize for her husband. Her embarrassment only increased when they went to a remote pond to swim. Compared to her friends, her husband was woefully out of shape, and, never having swum nude before, he couldn't stop joking. The more he talked the less her friends talked, until by the end of the weekend her friends were almost silent. When they finally headed back to the city in the BMW—which now looked opulent compared to her friends' battered Volkswagen—she sat in angry silence.

At the least her vanity was hurt. Though in the political world few men were more impressive than her husband, measured by the standards of those living simple physical lives he was hopelessly inadequate, and, worse, unable to grant such lives space to exist around him. He had been a lout.

Much as she was taken with the rural calm, however, she was glad to be heading home. In the city, after all, important things were getting done, and they were at the center of it all. Yet for the first time she wished her husband less competitive, less rigid, less bureaucratized. Less himself. It did not soothe her when, sensing her unspoken criticisms, he began to mock her country friends.

As if to compensate for her thoughts, which she considered disloyal, she began almost without knowing it to defer to his judg-

Who Wrote the Book of Love?

ment. Returned a sofa he didn't like. Phoned friends and canceled a dinner when he didn't want them to come over. Gave way whenever it seemed important to him to prevail. Much as all this pleased her husband, in terms of restoring her original feeling for him it was not an entirely effective strategy: the more she yielded the more peremptory he became. Or he would patronize her, explaining a political struggle, for example, as if she couldn't possibly understand.

As more time passed he was under enormous stress from work, and even the attention he received—magazine articles, several prizes, an honorary degree—only took more time, more travel. They saw each other little, made love seldom. Speaking with her parents or friends, she occasionally hinted that she was displeased with the marriage, but carefully avoided blaming her husband, speaking rather of the pressures of his job, saying that a vacation would set things right.

In this period she began to resent driving him to and from the airport, not simply because he seemed to take her services for granted ("You're not doing anything, are you?" was how he'd put it), but because she'd come to abhor both the drive and the airport itself. All those cars on the freeway, going where? And all those planes hurdling so many miles at crazy speeds. Though he told her she was acting like a child, she was adamant in refusing to accompany him on any more of his work trips. She was beginning to want to function more simply, the road and the airport now epitomizing the aspect of urban life she wanted to distance herself from. And, increasingly, the aspect of her husband she wanted to distance herself from.

One night they were entertaining a group of foreign monetary experts. Just back from a long flight, totally exhausted, her husband kept addressing one official by his predecessor's name. Far down the table, increasingly exasperated, she repeatedly tried to get her husband's attention, but, engrossed as usual in what he was saying, he never noticed. She thought she'd explode.

Still angry the next morning, when a friend called she told her what had happened, not only giving the specifics but making no effort to excuse or soften her husband's error. When she hung up, she realized that it was the first time she had spoken against her husband to anyone. It didn't make her feel bad. Taking stock of her anger, she decided that most of all she was enraged at herself. She had made a terrible error. He had always been a boor.

That afternoon the doorbell rings. Delivery man with a package. Young, hip, laughing, eager to talk. No, he knows nothing about politics. Likes to ski and—smoke dope. How her husband would sneer. A hippy! As she continues to talk with the delivery man, she asks him if he'd like to share a joint back in the garden. Yes he would, he really would.

This is the night, then, that her husband comes home tired after another day of knocking heads at the office. Under the trees in the far corner of the garden she hears him pull into the driveway, slam the door of the BMW, enter the house, call "Anybody home?," and walk heavily back to the bedroom. "To watch Monday Night Football," she says to the delivery man, pulling him closer.

This is the universe they inhabit, one of a hundred on their street alone, but who could tell them it might be different, and who would live it for them? A steady routine: careers for both, the child, and the marriage, their Rock.

When he does something she has no use for, she stands there saying "That's my husband for you," irritated but never suggesting it isn't part of life as it's lived. Always serious before they married, now, between job and baby, her face is often tired and stern. The dog chases the postman and, after she closes it in the basement, won't stop barking; the baby almost falls down the stairs; her car gets a flat tire; her husband didn't pick up his dirty clothes: pieces of a whole. Old enough to have some idea of what, as she puts it, she's "in for," she appraises what might have been only to sleep in the bed she's sure she made for herself. "I never really knew any other man," she says, aware that times have changed but with so little sense of a realizable alternative that her voice is neither bitter, nor, even, wistful.

For his part, unwilling to molt, he's withdrawn within the fortress of his home, installing burglar alarms and safety glass as if to insist that the real threats are outside. "Decency," he often says, "there's just not enough common decency these days." Thinking, perhaps, of a courtly salute to the lady in distress, or sacrificing himself to save the wagon train. Decency. Equals abnegation. Not taking advantage. Of the lady.

Frequently he tells his wife that the house is about paid off, that if he dies she and the kid will be o.k. Far from being able to admit to himself that he wants a divorce, a perception of the outer world as hostile the strongest emotion he now shares with his wife, he looks to obligation and the future for his pleasures. Rigging an emergency fire ladder by the bedroom window, checking the long-handled ax in its brackets, he anticipates the praise of prudent others as they one day witness the precautions he took for his family's well-being. Two hundred thousand dollars of life insurance, the mortgage almost paid off too. "That was love," he hears—from the far side of the grave—them saying, "that really was love."

 "Till death do you part." That's the way she often thought it would be, long after the divorce, every time her former husband showed up for his weekly visit with the children. She felt she'd never be rid of him, at least not for the eternity until the kids were grown up.

Typically he came early, came late, or canceled his plans at the last minute, leaving her to disappoint the children. Or he'd arrive with his latest lover, usually someone very young, making her feel old and dowdy as she got the kids ready to go. He loved to buy them expensive toys to make her look cheap, but then he'd be weeks late with the child support money, complaining he was broke, forcing her to call him again and again, then telling her to stop badgering him. When it suited him, finally giving the money as though she had no right to it, as though, suddenly, they were *her* children. "You're bleeding me to death," he liked to say. At long last putting the folded bills into one of the kids' hands ("Go in and give this to your mother") as he dropped them off after some pointlessly lavish spree. She didn't have to hate him to get clear of what they had created between them, but he made it hard not to.

Even so, she'd remind herself, he was still the children's father. Over and again she bit her tongue when they were in front of the kids, determined to play fair in their presence. She could still remember how, years before, he stood up to her parents when they first went out, frank about his interest in her, unashamed and unabashed. And brave enough, not long after, to announce to her father that they were engaged. He simply rejected all her father's opinions and threats: "Your daughter is twenty now," he said forcefully, "old enough to make her own decisions." Though it had been his decision, in which she concurred, though she hadn't really believed it could be done. He took her away from home in his sports car—"a dangerous luxury," she could still hear her father calling it—and as they drove off she felt free for the first time in her life. Now, years later, she could still thank him for that at least.

When things soured between them, she took the blame. He'd given up a fine job with Blue Cross to go into the health care business for himself. She should have stopped him, particularly since he kept saying he was doing it for her. After months of tension and fear the company was just holding its own, and seemed unlikely to improve. The whole effort had been pointless. But for too long in the marriage she'd been hard on him—as if, through her, her father still called the tune—just as she'd been too severe with their first child. Perhaps, responding to her expectations, her husband had tried to impress her. A bad idea, in any case: he worked long hours now, earned little money, felt like a failure. Twelve years married, seeing him struggle, she was full of regrets.

When he suggested a trial separation, she was afraid of losing him, but as she started dating—he'd been seeing other women for months, often pressing her to loosen up and take a lover—he went crazy, beating her, threatening to leave the state with the children. Initially intimidated, still feeling guilty, slowly she gained her distance from him.

Down to the morning of the divorce he contrived to procrastinate the hearings, repeatedly failing to appear in court after she had again jeopardized her job by taking another day off, advising her through his attorney that he'd contest custody of the children by documenting her "unfit moral behavior." He scared her with that, and she stopped going out for a while.

But finally they were both in the courtroom. "She called me and said that her husband had just thrown a kettle of boiling water at her," her sister testified calmly, "and she was very upset, crying over the phone." Of course it hadn't happened that way. Would that it had been so simple, some single act pushing them over a precipice clearly marked "Divorce." But this was law, not life; the court required a formula before granting a decree. "Something like boiling water is very good," her lawyer had told her, "if your sister will swear to it."

The lawyers huddled with the judge up at the bench out of her hearing. "He'll agree to drop the moral behavior issue, in essence making divorce possible today, on two conditions," her lawyer came back to tell her. "First, no alimony."

"I've told him and I've told you all along, I don't want alimony," she said angrily.

"Keep your voice down," her attorney whispered. "That's fine, just fine. The other condition is that he pay only a hundred dollars a month for child support."

"A hundred dollars a month? For four children?"

"I know it's less than he should offer," her lawyer whispered, "but otherwise he insists he'll fight you all the way, and that could take quite a while."

"How long is quite a while?"

"A year, maybe more. You never know."

"All right, all right. Agree to his terms. I just want it to be over."

"You sure? You know what this means?"

"What choice is there?"

She went out into the gray winter day a single woman, and spent the next few hours alone, just walking. Finally, her feet long since cold and wet from the slush, she got into her car, some of her anger gone, still trying to impose order on all that had happened. "It'll take me some time to work out," was the best she could manage.

Her life as a divorcée was incredibly hectic. After she packed the children off to school in the morning, always a photo finish, she worked a full day as a social worker, did the shopping, came home to pay the baby-sitter, prepared dinner, cared for the inevitable daily catastrophes, got the children tucked into bed, and then, even when totally exhausted, went out as often as she could. She was determined to get back into the flow of life, to meet another—and better—man.

She suffered all the normal pratfalls: fell in love with a married teacher who, after endless agonizing, wouldn't leave his wife; dated an attractive high school baseball coach who was, finally, determinedly single; spent several months seeing a doctor who loved her but loathed children. The doctor even proposed, but she never really gave it a thought: she just couldn't imagine how he could be part of their family. In the wake of this relationship she became depressed. What, after all, were the odds on a single woman of thirty-three with four children finding a husband? Jimmy the Greek would just laugh. But for all the pressures and all the mistakes, still she felt herself coming alive again. The world wasn't the orderly place she once thought it was, but she felt better to know she could survive.

One night at a coffeehouse she met a quiet physicist who was also a folk music buff. It was hootenanny time, and he took the stage when his turn came, playing the guitar earnestly but so badly that she had to stifle a laugh. Several nights later he called and asked her out. Soon they were dating regularly.

Though for some time he hardly overwhelmed her, she found him candid and at ease with himself. Far from avoiding the kids, he enjoyed their company, seemed to take it as a given that they were part of her life. He'd had some rough times of his own, including a hard separation from his wife, but seldom wasted much time on self-pity or bitterness. There was a hard-won truthfulness in him which only grew on her. Nor did he bat an eye when her ex-husband came by to make a scene. Without compromising himself, he seemed to take it as a matter of course that people had pasts, possibly unpleasant pasts, yet never measured her except by what they had experienced between them.

What with jobs, commuting, errands, and the children, they had little time alone together, but instead of drifting apart or taking their anger out on each other, they slowly drew closer. Late at night, sharing one of the exotic drinks he liked to mix, they'd get tipsy and laugh at themselves and the world, always concluding with a toast they had discovered one drunken evening.

"To those who see straight lines in a crooked world," he'd say, "not to belittle curves, of course, beggin' your pardon."

Who Wrote the Book of Love?

"Little curves? Well, then, to lovers and other fools," she'd answer as they emptied their glasses.

There were never fewer than a thousand possible grounds for going their separate ways. He got very sick for several months. She was fired from work and worried incessantly about money until, after weeks of anxiety, she found another job. And both former spouses seemed bent on doing all they could—short of collaborating—to make life unpleasant for them. The late-night drinks helped, they savored the quiet after the children were finally in bed, but nothing would have sufficed had not a genuine trust developed between them. She marveled at how seldom, even in the most confused moments, they attacked each other. The word "courtesy," which sounded almost archaic to her ear, kept occurring to her. It wasn't "manners" or "politeness" he was showing her: it was a steady respect she had never before been accorded.

Despite the hurly-burly of their lives, he too was at peace with himself, and together they only grew stronger. It was perhaps this newfound calm after so many storms which explains why they started putting on weight. Of course she was eating too many sweets and he had recently stopped smoking, but it went beyond that. Food was simply one pleasure they didn't have to deny themselves. Eating at a restaurant, beyond the reach of phones and calamities, they could be alone and have someone care for them for a change. They went out as often as they could afford to, buying drinks before dinner, wine with the meal, liqueur after. Time passing, standing in the bathroom together checking the scale, not believing the dial, or just looking at each other, they had to laugh.

They laughed on the day of their wedding, too, having overslept in a preconjugal bed, scrambling madly to get dressed, swerving from side to side through the unplowed snow to get to the church. When they finally arrived, it seemed to her that her whole life was passing before her eyes. Except for her former husband, who wasn't in the room?

There was her father standing off to the side, glowering, still certain his daughter had wasted her life, determined as always to let her know it.

"Let him go to the grave that way, if that's how he wants it," she said to her husband-to-be. "I'm not going to shed any more tears."

"Neither am I, then," he answered, pulling her tight. But she did almost cry to see the kids, his and hers, one—if only one—with his arm in a cast, all with white shirts dirty long before the wedding anthem.

Standing in the congregation were their friends, a number of them, of course, their former lovers. Her sister, still calm, was also there, as was her attorney. "Not whispering now," she thought to herself. The doctor who had once proposed to her was busy taking wedding pictures. And her husband-to-be's ex-wife, in an attempt to establish a better relationship with them, had insisted on doing all the catering for the reception.

So there they were in the old church, now almost man and wife, venerable bearded former ministers looking sternly down at them from their frames on the wall, organ rumbling, guests shifting restlessly in their pews. The lights were dimmed. Holding their candles, the children formed a circle, and then everyone joined in to sing "Amazing Grace":

>I once was lost, but now I'm found,
>Was blind, but now I see.

 From the time they were married they did little partygoing, nor did they often seek out others for socializing. Tacitly they agreed that after his days at the hospital—he was a biochemist—and hers at the juvenile home—she was a counselor—they had had enough of people. Not that they didn't like both their jobs and their colleagues, but after work they welcomed the quiet of their home and each other's company. Particularly walking through the snow to get the paper and some sweet rolls on winter Sundays, then returning home to savor the warmth, they appreciated how comfortable they were with each other, remembered how very glad they were to have met. The radiator clanked; the days passed slowly.

They'd been married several years when she decided to see a psychiatrist. Far from having to straighten out something in their relationship, she felt that being so secure freed her to explore and make better accommodation with some bitter childhood experiences.

Trusting, as usual, his wife's judgment, her husband encouraged her even though the psychiatrist most highly recommended would be expensive. He knew that her upbringing had been tough, and admired his wife for wanting to expose it to light and understanding.

The psychiatrist told her she could see him only if she would commit herself to a two-year program, four meetings a week. Since she worked and the doctor already had a full late-afternoon and evening schedule, she agreed to have her sessions at seven A.M. Her husband was somewhat startled by the proposed regimen: she'd have to rise very early, make the long drive to the doctor's office, see him, work a full day, and then retire early. In addition, the cost of so many sessions would absorb most of her earnings, setting back for a while their hope of buying a home. In spite of these reservations he gave his approval.

The first few months she was in therapy seemed well worth the investment of time and money. She told her husband she was gaining access to some painful memories and was certain to profit emotionally in the long run. At the same time, he noticed that she was increasingly fatigued. Often unable to force herself to get to sleep early, she still had to rise by five-thirty in order to reach the doctor's office on time. When her husband suggested that perhaps she cut her job down to half time, she insisted that she then wouldn't have enough money for the doctor, and that if she worked less she'd lose all hope of promotion. Seeing how exhausted she was, her husband for the first time wished she hadn't decided to see the psychiatrist.

A month later she came down with the flu. She missed work for several days and canceled her appointments with the doctor, but then, still not fully recovered, resumed her heavy schedule. Noticing how much weight she had lost, beginning to be very worried about the strain on her, her husband again urged her to cut down in some way, but again she refused. Thinking it over, her husband finally decided to call the psychiatrist.

"Hello, doctor," he said. "As you know, my wife has been your patient for about six months now."

"Yes," the doctor replied.

"Well, what I'm calling about is to say that I'm concerned that the combination of work and the early-morning appointments is putting her under too much stress, and I wonder if you have any suggestions."

"I don't know quite what you have in mind," the doctor replied.

"For instance, doctor, could you meet her at another time of day, since I think that having to get up so early is causing her to lose sleep."

"No, that's impossible. My schedule is quite full already, and I see no way to shift it around."

"Then how about seeing her somewhat less often? Would that make an enormous difference?"

"I'm afraid it would. I don't think I could recommend that."

"But when my wife came to you she had no particular disability, just a desire to work some things through."

"That's quite correct, but something important may well be at stake for her now, and she and I have made a contract to facilitate just that kind of process. Both the frequency of meeting and the guarantee of regularity are what create the possibility of progress."

"That makes good sense to me, doctor, but the life she's leading now, between working and having her appointments, seems to me to be exacting a price on her that may be greater than whatever strain she was under before therapy began."

"Are you suggesting that your wife shouldn't be seeing me?" the doctor asked, sharply.

"Not at all, not at all," her husband replied, startled by the doctor's tone. "I'm simply trying to say that my wife is not looking well, nor has she looked well for several months, and that I think the source of her not looking well at this moment seems to be not so much psychic as physical. I'm hoping that you, as her doctor, will take cognizance of this."

"Well," the doctor said more calmly, "if you're really concerned, perhaps I could give her something to help her sleep better at night."

"That seems a rather indirect solution to this human problem," her husband replied. "Surely this is the kind of situation that can be better solved on its own terms, don't you think?"

"I'm afraid I can't be of any help to you in the way you suggest. I happen to believe that it is most important for your wife that we continue things as they are. And, frankly, if I were you, I'd reexamine your motives for this call."

Her husband was stunned. The conversation had got completely out of hand, and he saw no way to set it straight.

"Well, doctor," he said, "that is most unkind of you. I had thought it all somewhat simpler, more mechanical. But thank you for speaking with me anyway."

When his wife returned home after her next session with the doctor, she was crying mad.

"You called my psychiatrist," she said to her husband, accusingly.

"Yes, I did," he replied quietly.

"What did you say to him?"

"I told him I thought you were overextended, physically, between working full time and your sessions with him. I was hoping that by explaining what I saw to him he might either change the time you met or else see you a little less often."

"What right did you have to do that?" she said bitterly.

"What right?"

"Yes. What right did you have to call my psychiatrist?"

"Hey, take it easy. I didn't mean to intrude in your life. I'm your husband, remember? I simply don't want to see you so overwhelmed that the cure becomes worse than the disease."

"It's not a disease!" she shouted at him. "I'm not sick."

"For Christ's sake," he said, "I didn't mean it that way. Calm down."

"You had no right!" she shouted again, and stormed back to the bedroom, slamming the door.

Time passing, she continued to look worn, but still she maintained her schedule. Weekends now were less pleasurable for them both; the issue of her seeing the psychiatrist had come between them, and neither could find a way back to the place they had shared before. Perhaps oversensitive because of her exhaustion, or, as likely, because of the intense feelings she was working through with the doctor, she couldn't forgive her husband for intruding into what was for her so private, for not supporting her fully in her choices. For his part, dating the tension in their relationship from the day she first saw the psychia-

Who Wrote the Book of Love?

trist, he feared that soon there would be only hurt and hostility between them.

Hoping that going away might bring them closer together, he fought with his lab director for an extra vacation, and considered himself lucky to be granted one for two weeks in the early summer. Returning home that evening, he told his wife about his plan: they'd go to the ocean.

"It sounds good to me," she said, "but I have to see what the doctor says."

"You do?" he asked.

"Certainly. I have a contract with him."

"Doesn't he take vacations?"

"I assume so. At the end of the summer, I think."

"But I had to fight to get anything. I can't get one then."

"Well, I'll ask him, but I don't know what he'll say. You have to remember that the doctor and I have a contract. He doesn't renege on it, and I can't either."

"But we have a contract too," her husband said, frustrated by this now inevitable presence in their relationship. "Or have you forgotten it, and that it came before your contract with the doctor?"

"That was a cheap thing to say," his wife replied. "That was a very cheap thing to say."

"I'll tell you this!" her husband shouted. "If that's your response, then we might as well plan on divorce. Talk *that* over with your doctor."

Late at night, unable to sleep, watching his wife toss and turn, seeing her exhausted and drawn face, her husband shook his head as if to shake off all that had come between them. But nothing changed: he was no closer to deciding whether it was his concern or his rage he should be more ashamed of.

South wind coming up hard and fast, both of us down to check our boats. Finding the lines secure, we stand by his bow making small talk.

"I teach college now," he says. "Easy job, no big money of course, but I've done a little of just about everything else. This at least is fairly honest, though the students are dumb." He laughs a warm laugh, as if appreciating the humor of the dumbness of the students, the strangeness of actually being paid to try to teach them.

"What else have you done for work?" I ask.

"Well, for a while I was a stockbroker, and then I went into the appliance business. Basically, you could say I ran a bait and switch racket, mostly on blacks. But let me tell you this, compared to being a stockbroker it was honest work." Again he laughs, and once more with the same quality of distance, as if savoring the fate that led him in such odd directions.

He looks at his boat. "I'm going to try going out solo tomorrow if the weather clears. Wife's staying home with the kids. They're still really too young to sail."

"It won't be long," I say, "and then you'll have plenty of free crew available."

"Maybe, maybe," he says, smiling, "but you never know. They might not like the boat, or we might be fighting. You just never know." He laughs once more. "The wife and I were going to go to Greece and buy a boat there, sail it in the Aegean summers, but first prices rose like crazy over there and then we had the kids. That was it as far as the money went."

"I'll bet."

"Got any of your own?"

Who Wrote the Book of Love?

"Not so far."

"This is my second crop," he says, laughing. "Once wasn't enough."

"I thought your wife looked young, considering all your gray hairs."

He laughs. "Yeah, she's nearly twenty years younger than I am. I have three kids by the first wife, and now two with the second. But I'll tell you, much as I love my kids, if you don't have any you just can't believe the expenses. Right there went the boat in Greece, even without the inflation."

"Well, since you already had children in your first marriage, how come you had these?"

"Hell," he laughs, watching his boat strain at the lines. "My second crop? You don't decide these things, even if you think you do. They just happen."

In the spring of 1950, turning fifteen on the farm in Montana, no longer willing to bear the scrutiny of her Mormon foster parents who, from the time she approached puberty, scrutinized her every movement for signs of her mother's genes, she walked twenty-two miles through the night to the train station. Early the next morning she headed south to San Francisco to search for her mother the whore.

Finding her mother an aging alcoholic stranger who told her to go back where she came from, she determined to stay. Living in a rented room and working as an usher in a movie house, finishing high school, she enrolled in the university. Quickly meeting campus radicals, responding to their zeal, for the next four years she picketed nonunion industries, demonstrated against the House Un-American Activities Committee, protested the loyalty oath. Often broke, someone she loved always in court, still she felt she had finally come home.

Just completing her studies, she met a young doctor who was also devoted to "the people." A short, powerful man, always in motion, skilled pathologist, linguist, singer, and athlete, he dazzled her. Despite the shadow of a year-long FBI investigation—he had gone to grade school with a now famous Communist, among other sins—they married.

As time passed, perhaps tired of always another set of martyrs, more defense funds, rent parties, and trials, her husband became more conservative. They argued often, among other things about her unwillingness to return to the university for a higher degree. Advancing rapidly in medical social life, her husband wanted someone he could show off, someone with credentials or at least a pedigree. She drove him wild by referring to herself as a "bastard child" when his colleagues asked about her background; by saying she came from a long

Who Wrote the Book of Love?

line of "scrabblefarmers"; by listening attentively to the woes of yet another of life's stragglers. Not about to change, even after eight years of marriage and two children, she told her husband he'd have to leave her behind if he was so eager to get ahead. They separated.

Working full time since she would take no alimony, caring for the children, she was surprised to discover that a principal pleasure in her life was her new home. Though mortgages for single women were then hard to come by, she'd finally been able to make the purchase. If initially she regarded the house simply as an economy, paying herself instead of the landlord, in time she came to value it as a refuge from the outside world. She didn't admire her need for such distance, nor was she entirely comfortable with the idea of ownership, but the home gave her happiness: it was hers.

One night, more than a year after their divorce, her former husband invited her out to dinner. They talked about mutual friends, the days when they first met, the children, his career, each taking the measure of how much had been lost when they separated. He had roses for her, told her more than once how beautiful she looked, was clearly trying to recover the best that was between them, and she felt tempted to pick up on his unspoken suggestion that they try it again. Who would she ever know as well? Who else had shared all that time? They cried that night when they made love, but the morning after he was all business as he put on his clothes, in her eyes quickly transforming himself into a man too hungry for success, too much in need of the confirmation of powerful others. Wearing a suit that was just too damn expensive. And as she dressed, she caught him looking at her as if still wondering why in hell she had to be so stubborn. He was family, she knew, one of them would be there to bury the other when the time came, but that was all.

Meanwhile other couples in her circle were divorcing, and more than one ex-husband came by to cry on her shoulder. She understood pain, they said, and she did, though with somewhat more distance than she'd felt when she was younger. She had heard the same stories too many times, understood that blame had to be shared, couldn't pretend not to know that for some misery there could be no solace.

One of these divorced men, by no means the most compelling, kept returning to visit her even after he regained his footing. He had never thought much one way or the other about social causes, but was a good musician, loved jokes, cooked fine food. "We could look out for each other," he said.

She felt a fool. He was no one to marry. She wanted some deep commitment, some grace, some faith. But she was also tired of being alone, she needed someone there at night. Maybe she was asking too much. She remembered the animals on the farm in Montana, just coupling.

In this period she fell in love from afar with a young man who worked in her office. Genuinely open to life, eager for experience, undaunted by the criticisms of the older staff, he reminded her of radical friends at the university ten years before. The night he quit his job he came by her house to celebrate. Drunk on wine, against her better judgment, at his initiative, they made love. The next morning, early, he was gone. Knowing she wouldn't see him again, feeling thirty and foolish, she called in sick and sat alone with a bottle of bourbon. Not until she put on Al Hibbler singing "Don't Get Around Much Any More" did she begin to smile.

Months passing, when the divorce proposed a second time, she spent a weekend thinking it over and then accepted. At the wedding, however, she still had her doubts. Looking around at the familiar faces she couldn't help but see it was the second time around. But things changed, she thought; she'd just have to accept that. Some people were stronger than others, some had more clarity than others, but the absolutism was long gone. "Truth," "justice," "the struggle," these words were no longer the vocabulary of their lives. Or hers. Laughter, music, decency, just a body next to hers, perhaps this would be enough. Without it, in any case, she was only growing older. Her mother had died before they ever really spoke to each other, and she

Who Wrote the Book of Love?

still had no idea who her father was, if her mother had even known. No, you couldn't get everything you wanted. You had to learn to take what life gave you.

Several days after the wedding her new husband moved his things into her house. She hadn't realized he owned so much. Racks of records, clothes, power tools, musical instruments, hi-fi components, gear for magic tricks, boxes of bric-a-brac, sports equipment, books, furniture.

Her kids were enthralled by so many possessions. She had to admonish herself—even as she was startled by so much that was his, thinking back to the poverty of her childhood on the farm—to be less severe. Though he wasn't yet aggressive enough physically for her, they *were* both laughing, and the kids seemed pleased. She thought it would work out all right. She made room for his things.

That afternoon he moved a soft chair into the living room. Right after he had carefully positioned it, just so, in the corner, her boy walked over to the chair and sat down to try it out. "No, no, not there," she heard her new husband say. "That's my chair."

She couldn't believe her ears, but there was no taking the words back. For the next few months she measured needs against wants, she tried the mathematics of small pleasures canceling out large hopes, she balanced what was at hand against what was beyond reach. But then one day as they argued, again hearing his words in her ears, willing now to settle for no more than what was hers, she said to her new husband: "Out, out, out of *my* house."

 From a poor family, his father a tailor, Al considered himself lucky to get a scholarship to a fine men's college. Though he excelled in his course work, he was often lonely, and studied as much for want of something better to do as for the rewards achievement might bring. He would have enjoyed the presence of women, but the nearest coeds were miles away; dating was for weekends, hours of driving through the snow. During the week, time to kill, he jogged and skied.

Getting his degree, having saved a little money by waiting on table, Al started to realize his dream of wandering through Europe, but the draft forced him home and back into school after two months. While interesting, studying law meant three more years in the kind of competitive environment he'd come to loathe. If he was angry that life had closed in, it was his style to stick it out: he was always skeptical of risk. Soon law school would be over, and then, he hoped, he'd have time to explore.

Anne came from a middle-class family that was always short of money. Speaking about growing up, she often criticized her parents for having seven children. Had there been fewer, she seemed to be saying, each would have had enough. An awkward if bright adolescent, she didn't come into her own until college.

Her posture was bad, her features irregular, but with long legs and a lean figure she was a very attractive young woman. Self-possessed and quick with words, eager for life, capable of both sharp insight and great warmth, she was sought out by many men. Now apparently compensated for any earlier deprivation, still she had enormous hungers, always ready for the admiration of others, the next party, more celluloid jewelry and flapper dresses.

Anne and Al met at a student-faculty dinner just before he

Who Wrote the Book of Love?

started his last year of law school, as she was finishing college. That night he heard her before he saw her.

"You don't mean to suggest that the husband shouldn't have left his wife, do you?" she was saying to a professor.

"What I mean," he replied condescendingly, "is that of course love implies obligation."

"No doubt it does, professor, but could you explain to me just how?"

The professor was becoming impatient. "I believe it is self-evident. In this context—a husband abandoning his wife and child—we needn't get too speculative about it. Obviously he should have been bound by the love he presumably once pledged."

"Incredible," she exclaimed, laughing, "the notion that love is in some way connected to action. But even if it is, shouldn't we ask first whether the obligation you speak of was explicit or implicit? And, if implicit, whether both parties were truly aware it existed?"

"My dear young girl," the professor retorted, exasperated. "Forget all your quibbling. A faculty member abandoned his wife and child. I hardly call that love, and, furthermore, I find it odd to hear you—a woman—defending such behavior."

"So I gather," Anne responded. "You might, however, find it less odd if you weren't so eager to dismiss my 'quibbling.' Think about it for a moment. Love's an emotion, a feeling. How can a mere feeling ever imply the existence of an imperative? Or, even if love does somehow imply obligation, when one stops loving doesn't the obligation cease? X simply no longer loves Y. Besides, one can have obligation without love. Why not, then, love without obligation?"

"We could philosophize this way for hours," the professor said angrily.

"And perhaps even learn something," Anne shot back. "But in any case, I personally believe that there's a 'love' which has nothing to do with bargains or actions. A 'love' that might, in this case, even keep a man with his wife and child."

"Incredible," Al thought. Having escalated the discussion, then reversed her field, she'd emerged as the champion of "true" love, this while implying that her opponent would never be adequate to such emotion, not with her, anyway. An inflammatory argument, coming from a lovely woman, particularly one wearing next to nothing under her skimpy knit dress. She hadn't fought fair, Al knew, but the fool deserved no better. She'd been magnificent.

Waiting to introduce himself, he noticed that she had little to say to the other women present. Still holding forth, surrounded by admiring men, nipples pressing at the fabric of her dress, she wasn't about to share the moment. She'd come to conquer.

When Al finally got to speak with her, he mentioned her argument with the professor.

"Oh," she said, smiling. "Such an unhappy man, don't you think? I have to learn to laugh at people like that. Sometimes life's just too serious to be taken seriously."

"But you do believe in love?" Al asked, grinning.

"With a capital 'l'? Of course. Isn't that clear? What else is there?"

Even after they were seeing each other regularly, Al couldn't help fearing she would leave him. Emphatically independent and still close to former lovers, Anne appeared quite capable of being on her own. Yet there she was, with him.

He felt no full commitment from her until tragedy struck: her younger sister was lost at sea in a boating accident. Shattered, full of guilt, Anne had terrifying nightmares for weeks, crying out again and again in her restless sleep that her sister was drowning. Always Al was there to comfort her, wiping her face with a cloth, giving her sedatives, tucking in the blankets, keeping watch. He had never seen such suffering, wanted more than anything to spare her such pain. Often she woke in the middle of the night, sobbing, holding him, begging him not to go. "I won't leave you," he'd say, kissing her. "I won't ever leave you."

Slowly she recovered, and finally seemed to be herself again. Taking a vacation together, skiing every day, making love each night,

Who Wrote the Book of Love?

they were both full of joy. Soon they were planning to marry. Though a wedding was surely appropriate to their happiness, it seemed a little strange at the time, for among their peers there was then little concern with traditional forms. Both Anne and Al said the ceremony was for their parents. As for themselves, if their feelings changed, they'd part.

It was a huge wedding. After the ceremony, family finally departing with last embraces and blessings, Anne drank champagne with her friends. "Marriage is a perversion of natural faithful affections," she said, laughing. "It's filled with hoaxes, falsehood, and guilt." Al laughed too. They were both very happy.

In the months that followed, the established order had ever less legitimacy in the campus community. No possibility now beyond reach, their friends increasingly defined themselves in terms of great causes. Moved by this public flux, Anne became restless with school. Though she was too interested in aesthetics to make any substantial commitment to social change, this was a moment when even to take drugs seemed a political assertion, when even the Left was swept aside by the rediscovery of license. It was this repudiation of the past and invitation to passion that moved Anne most.

Meanwhile Al struggled to hold himself in check. A little longer, a little longer, and he'd be done. Law school was now worse than boring; at best attorneys seemed to be playing an outmoded and repressive game. Yet Al was on his own and knew it. The question of how to make a living was hardly the burning issue of the day, but he wondered what, if not law, he could do.

They'd been married no more than a year when Anne took a lover. Knowing Al would be devastated, she saw it as no small step. Yet the times were changing; all around her were men of restless raw power. She told Al that, not seeking it out, she'd fallen in love, that though she still loved him she was prepared to accept whatever decision he made. But because he himself yearned for more freedom, because her feelings were real, her confusion genuine, and because he simply wasn't ready to live without her, Al said he understood. When her lover soon left town, carried off by some new cause, Anne wept and Al sighed with relief. They resumed life as before.

Within months it seemed that the revolution was imminent, but already Al had moved up north to a remote town to take a job. Still in the city, to follow when she completed the course work for her master's, flattered by the attention of men she wanted to know better, inspired by the dreams around her, Anne denied herself nothing.

Given the times, no one she knew save her parents—and the part of herself they spoke for—would have disputed her desire to live as she wanted. But what, then, of Al? Wrestling with possibilities, she reasoned that she loved him no less, that, in fact, the richer her life the more she'd bring to him. Plural marriages, group sex, and free love now common in her community, these arguments didn't sound entirely implausible. Yet she doubted one could play it both ways, spoke sadly of separation, wistfully of accommodations that might be made. Al, meanwhile, was alone and working hard, still sending her money to finish school. Waiting for her, receiving her long letters, he thought she'd leave him.

Finally arriving, happy to see him, still Anne wasn't sure she'd stay. Cleaning house, shopping, running errands, isolated and resenting the drudgery, she kept noticing the many "freaks" doing odd jobs, dealing dope, living on welfare. She began to press Al to loosen up, to take more time off, saying he was a fool to spend so much time at the office. "What about pleasure?" she'd keep asking, certain his job was work, work *prima facie* painful.

He refused to listen. Despite the confining routine, he liked solid wages after so many years of scrimping. And though being an attorney was far from tapping the wild energy of the times, it was something he did well, even an opportunity to help others. Perhaps also, fearing he could neither keep Anne nor keep up with her, he sought out structure all the more.

So there they were, a couple, taxpayers, amortizing school debts while all around them people were openly "ripping off" the system. And because Al had little energy left after work, they usually paid cash for every good and service. House repairs, car repairs, medi-

Who Wrote the Book of Love?

cal bills, food, clothing: the money went out as fast as Al earned it.

Given Anne's dissatisfaction with such middle-class traps ("I don't think two is the perfect number," she told Al), their separation seemed imminent. But instead, blaming him for not spending more time with her, she began seeing other men, leaving for a night at a time, returning the next morning.

Sick at heart, Al said nothing. Perhaps he thought himself unnecessarily "uptight." The world had changed. How set the limits? Perhaps he believed negotiation impossible, that it would be Anne's terms or none at all. Or perhaps, whatever she did, he couldn't abandon the Anne he'd nursed when her sister had died.

Had he merely pretended strong interest in another woman, Anne might well have come home to stay if that was the goal. But Al couldn't play the game, didn't see it as a game, much less as war. Nor did it occur to him that alone he might find safer ground. As if believing that she had some special claim on life, he gave way.

Now only one of several men she loved, Al was still her husband, a professional man, crux of the life she felt she'd been told to live. Though she passionately advanced theories and admonitions about living for freedom and love, the real debate, which she had yet to resolve, was within herself. At each critical point, however, that internal argument reduced itself to resentment and anger. Who said she couldn't play it both ways?

Self-justification soon became her greatest labor. She liked to say, for instance, that Al chose to work. His earning power obviously greater than hers, it followed that there was no good reason for her to get a job. In fact, of course Al was too well paid for what he did. Were the world more fair, attorneys would earn far less, nothing at all if things were perfect.

A year of this married life passing, often alone for days at a time, Al began occasionally to spend the night with other women, always careful, however, to clear his choices with Anne. "Now he's living for pleasure," she announced triumphantly. Though she set his limits, she needn't have bothered: Al complied with her terms as if the miracle was in sustaining their relationship. As in a way it was. He worked hard, she played hard, but the real nub of their lives was Anne's refusal to have less than all she wanted. Al's willingness to let her try, however—to bind her to him with guilt?—served her badly: without a counterforce she was increasingly self-deceived, ever more ruthless.

In time a new phenomenon presented itself. Though she seemed beyond the rule of that kind of gravity, Anne was rebuffed by one of her lovers. While it was the hallmark of her relations with other men that she never had to play for full stakes—being married, after all—nonetheless she found the rejection galling. She also began to fear that she might "jeopardize the marriage." Her apprehension increased when a jealous neighbor, an older woman, told her she wasn't getting younger, that she'd lose her husband unless she settled down.

One evening soon after she was out dancing. Seeing her flirting with other men at the bar, her companion of the evening pulled her out to the street, knocked her down, and drove off. Alone in the night with a black eye, sure that the day of reckoning had come, Anne wept her way home to Al. But two nights later she was gone again.

To counter her fears, Anne advanced still more argument, like a Ptolemaic astronomer adding epicycles, until language finally lost all meaning. Long since, for example, pleasure required a capital "p." Now, though it was probably too much to have her lovers come by when Al was home, as "friends" of course they'd always be welcome. And how many "friends" she had! No doubt it was, as she argued, for the best. If life gave each of us all the warm bodies we needed, surely there'd be fewer wars, fewer Trojan wars, in any case. But through it all Anne kept her hold on Al.

One Sunday they drove to the beach. There Anne suggested they take LSD, something she had done many times, Al never. Those experienced with drugs might have counseled against it: there was trouble between them, and Al had to be at work in the morning. But perhaps eager to catch up to the Freedom she so often spoke of, he was game. Soon Anne was in the water, riding the waves, surfing from one tide pool to another shrieking with laughter. Alone, up on the

Who Wrote the Book of Love?

beach, mutilating women of the night, Al was certain he was Jack the Ripper.

Shortly after this debacle Anne found a cottage of her own, though resentful of being the one to move. She would, she decided, see Al several days a week, "friends" the rest of the time.

By now they'd lived in the country nearly three years. More time passing, she allowed one of her lovers to move in with her, dividing most of her energy between him and Al, though insisting—to her lover, now—that of course she retained the right to do as she liked. Even with Al as an exemplum her lover couldn't see it. There was no question that Anne cherished him—who could be more tender?—but at the point of exacting parity from her he, like Al, was helpless.

Nearly twenty-six, Anne began to talk about having a child. Lover sitting silent through her deliberations, she finally decided that Al would make the best father. They were already married, after all, she loved him, and he'd be able to support a family. Al apparently acquiesced, continuing to give her money and gifts, but he seemed at long last weary of what they had created between them.

Finally, inevitably, Al met another woman. Though he no longer cleared his lovers with Anne, his relations with them had continued to have at least a component of being done for effect. Now, however, a real alternative existed. Her worst fear confirmed, Anne came to his office daily, badgering him, saying it was time for the child, time to go away together for a long vacation. But because he wanted revenge, or because he simply had finally found Pleasure, Al told her he wanted a divorce.

"You'll have to pay alimony," Anne raged, bringing him to tears. "No amount can be too much for what I'm suffering. I'll show you you can't abuse someone this way. I've given you the best years of my life. I'll stop you from doing the same to another woman."

Though she had always seemed untouched by time, ever capable of being nineteen again, there was suddenly no longer anything girlish about her. Hair cut short and curled, she took a part-time job and began to walk around town wearing a matronly dress and stockings, insisting on every bit of her age. And on something else. A working woman, that was her message, a woman struggling to make ends meet because she'd been wronged by her husband. Look what he had done! Al now lived with his lover as Anne did with hers. Though he continued to speak of divorce, months passed and still no papers were filed. Anticipating a reconciliation, Love triumphant, perhaps even a second honeymoon, Anne pointedly maintained her marital status and obligations. Sending a Christmas gift to Al's parents, for instance, she signed herself "Al's wife."

And so it persisted, the two of them living apart, but, still, husband and wife. Not quite as they were when they first met, world exploding with discovery, nothing beyond dreaming, but as they'd already spent the years: staving off separation, clinging to their marriage like sailors to a spar, ship long since swallowed by the sea.

 More than a century and a half after Lord Nelson said "ships and men rot in port," the captains of the yachts tied up at the quay waiting for the end of the hurricane season could only have confirmed his wisdom. Long since they had scraped and painted, tested rigging, sewn torn sails, restocked provisions, taken on fuel, whipped frayed line, scarfed extra fittings from abandoned boats, bartered with each other for what they couldn't jury-rig or buy. It was left only to wait for the southeast trades, the great determination that had launched them across the Pacific from the Galápagos or the Marquesas now steadily eroding in the muggy heat. They drank, womanized, bickered, worried about their diminishing funds. A nautical philosopher less august but no less acute than Lord Nelson said "boats are floating holes into which one endlessly pours money." Having braved the sea, these mariners now risked going down in harbor, victims of the unchartered but still dangerous shoals of Polynesian paralysis and wildly inflated island food prices.

The young captain of the thirty-two-foot ketch *Sea Foam,* bound single-handed around the world from San Francisco, was one day desultorily tinkering with self-steering gear he knew would never work properly when he heard a woman's voice as permission to come aboard. "Permission granted," he called, and turned around to see the tan and lithe crew member of *Resolute,* a thirty-eight-foot yawl. Though they had encountered each other often during the last month at taffrail parties and in bars on shore, she had never visited before. Much attracted to her, he had been unable to contrive a way to get to know her better without creating a stir in the tiny floating community.

"What brings you aboard?" he asked, smiling.

"Well," she said, "to be frank, I want to leave *Resolute*."

He took a moment to respond. Getting into a boat's crew problems was like walking into an argument between married people: an outsider could get hurt trying to help. Besides, she wasn't just *Resolute*'s crew. As he understood it, she was also sleeping with the captain.

"So what can I help you with?"

"Do you need crew?" she asked.

"Well, up to this point I've been sailing single-handed."

"Where are you going from here?"

"Cook Islands, New Zealand, and on around. No particular hurry."

"How's your money holding out?"

"Not so good."

"And what about the self-steering?"

"Unreliable for sure."

"Sounds like you need crew."

"I might at that."

"Particularly if your crew was someone like me. Wouldn't it make a long passage more human?"

"Much more human."

"I tell you what, then," she said, "I'll go fetch my seabag and bring it over. And that'll be that."

"Right now?" he answered, more than a little incredulous.

"Right now. Back in a flash."

A half hour later she rematerialized with her gear, stowed it forward, and disappeared again to do some shopping. "Crew's treat," she said, laughing, as she hopped onto the quay and headed into town.

Only moments after she left, *Resolute*'s captain appeared at *Sea Foam*'s gangplank, demanding and receiving permission to come aboard.

"My crew posted a notice saying she was moving to your vessel. I'm here to bring her back."

"I'm afraid you can't do that," *Sea Foam*'s captain said.

Who Wrote the Book of Love?

"Who the hell's going to stop me? You? Don't make me laugh."

"No," *Sea Foam*'s captain replied, eager not to let things get out of hand, "I'm not going to try to stop you, but to begin with she's not even here right now."

"That's all right. I'll just wait."

"Look," *Sea Foam*'s captain said, "this all probably looks different than it is. She just showed up here and asked if she could join the ship. If it hadn't been me, someone else would have said yes. You probably would have done the same thing in my place."

"I don't know what I would have done, but I know what I'm going to do. I'm taking her back. She belongs on *Resolute*."

"No doubt she does, but speaking man to man, I don't see how you can stop her. There are just limits on what you can do in a situation like this."

"Speak for yourself, dammit. I'll take care of this my way."

"All right, all right. But since we're both here waiting, why don't we have a drink?" *Sea Foam*'s captain went below and broke out some rum and two glasses, glad that at least for the moment there wouldn't be any craziness. Who knew where the fool thought he was coming from?

After *Resolute*'s captain had downed a number of shots, quickly showing the effects of the liquor, he said, "Between you and me, it's a rotten thing you did."

"Jesus Christ. Lay off, will you. She's the one to blame."

"Maybe so, maybe not, but personally I think it's a rotten thing you did to me," *Resolute*'s captain said, pouring himself another glass.

"Look, let's be reasonable. I agree that it's a rotten thing but she's a grown woman. She has the freedom to do what she wants to do. How can you fight that?"

"Shit, she has the right to do wrong. In one afternoon I've lost my crew and my woman."

"I can appreciate that. Hell, I've lost women too. But you get over it. Besides, you'll find new crew in no time."

"Not like her I won't. For one thing, she can navigate. For another, she's a qualified sailmaker. And for a third, she's a she. See what I mean?"

"I believe I do," *Sea Foam*'s captain replied, pouring them both another glass. "That is one hell of a loss."

"One hell of a loss is right. First right thing you've said. For a goddam pirate you did very well for yourself. Very well indeed."

"Come on, man, it wasn't piracy at all, can't you accept that?"

"To hell with accepting anything you say," *Resolute*'s captain replied, fumbling with the bottle of rum. "If you ask me, it was out-and-out piracy. Just murder. And I'm the only loser. I should show you what it's like. I should blow your goddam boat up, that's what I should do. That would fix you."

"Look," *Sea Foam*'s captain replied, "this is getting out of hand. I know you're a reasonable man, and I like to think I'm a reasonable man too. I still don't say this thing is really between us, but even so I happen to believe that when people lose something they should be compensated." He looked over at *Resolute*'s captain, who was now holding his head in his hands, muttering to himself. "What do you think?"

"About what?" *Resolute*'s captain said without looking up.

"About the idea that people should be compensated for loss." *Sea Foam*'s captain kept at this point somewhat unwillingly, but it did seem like a possible solution, particularly because he had no desire to keep watch night after night trying to protect his boat from some maniac. He'd have to go ashore sometime. All somebody had to do was cut the anchor line and he'd lose the vessel. Even so, the idea of compensation had risks; he had visions of having to stake his compass, life raft, or depth finder to achieve a settlement. Still, hoping to prevent something far more costly from happening, he stuck with the idea.

"Well," he said, "between us as skippers, as honorable men, what do you think would be fair in a situation like this, assuming it happened to two other people?"

Who Wrote the Book of Love?

Lifting his head, *Resolute*'s captain poured himself another shot, quaffed it, and sat shivering for several moments. Suddenly shoving his glass across the table, crashing it into the bottle of rum, he pushed himself up and out of the chair and wavered his way over to the gangplank.

"I'm going now," he said, blearily, his eyes unfocused. "I'm going right now. But I want you to know that I'm hurting. It may not look it, but I'm hurting very bad. This has been a rotten day for me, the worst day of my whole life."

"I know it has," *Sea Foam*'s captain said, "and I'm sorry about the whole thing. I hope we can part as friends, I really do. And I want to be sure you understand that I believe people should be compensated for such losses."

"You mean it?"

"I really mean it, more than I can say."

"You swear it?"

"I swear it, on my honor."

"I tell you what, then," *Resolute*'s captain said, unsteady on his feet, slurring his words. "I tell you what. How 'bout a couple dozen eggs?"

 He would have been hard pressed to precise what made him want to buy a house. Perhaps it began with the smog in the flatlands where they lived, particularly after the city diverted commuter traffic from shortcuts through neighborhood streets onto a main artery unfortunately close to the cottage they leased. Since they couldn't afford to rent up in the hills above the smog line, it made some sense to think about buying and fixing up a run-down house in an area they liked. Or he may have noticed, making out yet another monthly check to his landlord one night, multiplying it by twelve and then again by four or five, that he could have been paying all that money to himself.

Whatever the impulse for wanting his own home, it wasn't a bad thing that at thirty-three he was considerably older than his second wife. His first wife had left him because of his unwillingness to settle down, to "grow up," as she put it. If, however, he had once roamed far and wide, eyes lighting up at the mere mention of some foreign land, measuring his world in terms of islands, seas, and plateaus, he now felt, as the poet said, that he could scare himself with his own desert places. Though to think about owning a home suggested to him that his world had diminished, his second wife found the idea reasonable enough: she loved to make things, fix things, accumulate things. Having their own home seemed sensible.

The search wasn't easy. Real estate had tripled in value the last five years; now even a two-bedroom stucco was going for sixty thousand dollars. He winced to think of the monthly payments they'd have to carry, at least twice their rent, but on the other hand they'd have tax benefits and a growing equity, as well as the pleasures of the place itself. The more they looked, however, the more angry he was to think how easily he might have bought years before. Worse, the inflationary spiral made a mockery of all the small economies he had practiced.

One day their realtor called to say there was a tiny three-room cottage in a secluded area going for only thirty thousand dollars. It needed work, he told them, but the lot itself was worth nearly seventeen thousand. There was already a bid on it, but because the cottage was substandard both in size and construction, it seemed unlikely that the bidder would be able to arrange bank financing. If they could borrow enough for the large down payment, the owner would probably carry a note for the balance. He urged them to drive up and see it right away.

The neighborhood was unbelievably quiet, site of a former ranch, the old cattleman still living next door in what had once been the barn. As they inspected the cottage the old man came by to introduce himself. "My mother built this place, all by herself, for a friend paralyzed in the war," he told them. "She didn't want to see him go to a rest home. She cared for him ten years, feeding him, changing his linen, bathing him, turning him over several times a day. It may mean something to you if I say that never in all those years until he died did he have a bedsore."

The old man walked the property with them, talking about how much trillium there had been before the ivy took over, where the land was slide and where solid, pointing out the fruit trees—apricot, pear, plum, apple—showing them which were healthy and what care they'd need. He wouldn't be a bad neighbor, they both thought, not bad at all. And through the old bay laurel trees they could see clear down to the Bay. The house itself couldn't have been more modest, no more than living room, bedroom, tiny kitchen, and primitive bath, but it was charming, even more appealing given its low cost.

Nor did the obvious problems seem insurmountable. They could add on a room, perhaps something with two stories and lots of storage space. That would make a tremendous difference. Then they could open up the rear wall to enlarge the kitchen area, and cut windows into the roof for more light. And they could buy a wood stove instead of installing space heaters. Fuel would be no problem: they could haul logs down from the mountains each time they went camping.

Later that day they learned that the bid had in fact been withdrawn. Signing a check for the earnest money and handing it over to the realtor, he immediately suffered a bad case of buyer's remorse. Not that he didn't want the cottage, but look what he was tying himself into. Insurance, taxes, repairs, mortgage payments, the whole inevitable weight of the place, he who for so long had needed no more than his health and a pack on his back. Home ownership felt like just the kind of puddle a man could drown in. "Don't worry," the realtor told him, "you have a week to reconsider as you learn more about it. And you can't lose the deposit."

Bad news came fast. The termite inspector reported that the cottage was riddled with holes. And when the engineer met them up at the lot, he expressed surprise that they had asked him to come. "You don't need me for this," he said. "Basically the structure has value only if you plan to live in it as is. Or you could even rent it out, I suppose. But as soon as you apply for a permit to make improvements or additions, they'll condemn it."

One of their friends, a carpenter, also came up, and told them that they might be able to salvage the roof. But nothing more. "Look," he said, laughing. "No foundation, studs every four feet, plates rotted out, water leakage on the ceiling. This isn't even a shack."

Ever buoyant, the realtor told them it still had possibilities. If they bought the site and laid out another thirty or thirty-five thousand dollars—having talked down the asking price a little—they'd come out of it all owning a small house in a prime location without having spent much more than the cost of something ordinary in a less attractive neighborhood. And their place, the smallest in an expensive area, would have its value accelerated by the high prices of the surrounding homes. Nonetheless, the realtor conceded, it was of course not quite what they had thought it was, not really a house, actually little more than a very expensive building lot.

He found it painful to withdraw from the purchase. Already he had daydreamed about buying a piano now that they'd be really

Who Wrote the Book of Love?

settled, had told his wife he'd get the last of his gear out of storage, for the first time in years having everything he owned in one place. What with these plans and the renovations they had imagined, he felt as if something already theirs was being taken away.

On the way down from their last—and sad—visit to the cottage, they stopped at another listing the realtor had suggested. A small, dark house, new redwood shingles inflating the asking price another ten thousand dollars, neighboring homes crowding in one a postage-stamp back yard. They couldn't get out of there fast enough. Sixty-five thousand dollars.

So they were back to go. Minus a hundred and fifty dollars for the inspection reports.

That evening they went down to the Bay and walked out on the long fishing pier. Despite the cleansing north wind and the crescent moon setting over the Gate like Bojangle's smile, he was depressed. Just being up in the hills forced him to realize how much money it would take to live there, money he wasn't ever apt to have, money the lack of which he had never quite noticed because they lived simply and among friends who, like them, rented. Despite all the freedom life had granted him, despite his wife, friends, and the many richnesses available to him, all he could think of was that he wanted the calm and beauty of living in the hills for himself.

Seeing the houses, hearing the prices, understanding that they were beyond his means, all this catapulted him back to choices he had made long ago. Should he have been living differently all this time, earning more money, settling in sooner? Had he been a fool, had he failed to understand the game, was he now seeing the penalties for his actions?

While these questions rushed through his mind, his wife was nearby talking to a fisherman who had just hauled in a small leopard shark. Though disappointed about losing the cottage, she seemed undismayed, apparently assuming that something else would come along, or not minding at all if they had to move to the country to afford a place.

She was only several feet away, but he began to study her as if from a great distance. She had been a fine companion, had first traveled with him and then filled what homes they had with treasures. Plants, shells, rocks, nests, feathers. Fine meals. Love. She had shared and enhanced his life. He would have gone insane without her. But now, he thought, he was changing, even faster than he knew. He wished she had a source of income beyond the part-time jobs she took to pay her way. He wished she could bring as much to the purchase as he did. Then they could buy even in the hills.

Still looking over at her, he thought of the professional women he had once spent time with: filmmakers, lawyers, nurses, teachers. He thought of the kind of credit—not to mention savings—they must have had access to. He thought also of the heiress he had once lived with. In fact, he thought of all the women he had ever been close to who would have had the resources to help buy the house he now wanted.

As his wife continued to examine the leopard shark, waves breaking against the pilings, Pleiades running high overhead, he wished she had money, yes, he wished she had money. And, it occurred to him, since she had none he might be better off with someone who did.

Though surely they were always all around me, I never saw them until the end of a rainy winter, and really not until early one evening when at long last the sky cleared. And then, in the afterglow of the waning day, they came into my ken, came out like stars. An elderly woman walking home from market, pausing after achieving a block before attempting the next; two aged gnomes, him with cigar pulling the wife behind; a grandfather watching his heirs mortgage the home he paid for free and clear. And Rose. "Once an adult, twice a child," she cackled as she watered her garden, throwing snails out into the streets. Her six cats watching.

Rose's garden. Anemone, crocus, marigold, primrose, iris. ("Iris makes you believe in God, doesn't it," she said.) Hyacinth, foxglove, tigridia, gladiolus, scilla, hollyhock. Black tulip, Johnny-jump-up, nasturtium, sweet william, columbine, verbena, phlox. Campanula. Cosmos. African lily, regal lily, black lily of the Nile. Canterbury bells. Snapdragons. Bird-of-paradise. Forget-me-nots.

"The *crocus flowers* very early," she said that evening. "When I was a child I couldn't find the verb," she told me, laughing, reaching for her baseball cap to see if it was still there.

When I stopped by her garden the next morning I said: "Hi, Rose. The crocus flowers very early." She jumped. "How did you know that?" she asked. "That one always gave me trouble. Never could find the verb. Was I embarrassed!"

Rose approaching eighty, at long last on her own. Stacks of clippings, books, and records against the day she becomes a shut-in. Diet of bananas, peanut butter, pureed vegetables, and ice cream. Afraid of dozing off into a dreamless sleep never to wake.

And Rose in her garden. Dove in the birdbath. Blackbird zipping up to a phone wire to shake and preen. Robin catching a worm. "Goodbye, worm," Rose calls out.

"I'm kinda lost in the world now," she says, cars roaring by the garden. "Old as I am, I can't really separate the dreams from the reality." Two white butterflies dance past her. "This is living," she exclaims.

"When I was a little girl, I had a mammy, Aunt Ruth, and she used to tuck me in every night. One evening I wandered down in the Negro section and there was a colored woman singing, sitting in a chair on her lawn, just singing. The sun went down and I stood there transfixed, I just stood there looking through the paling. And then a colored man, Jim, he came along and opened the gate for me—the latch was too high to reach—and he said: 'Now you go tell your mama I let you in, and don't you ever be out this late again.'

"Once I embarrassed my mother. Lord! We were sitting at table, I couldn't have been but three or four, still in the high chair, and when everyone was ready for the prayer, I lifted up my small plate and said: 'Here, Grandpa, read my plate.' I thought that's where he got the prayer, I thought he read it off the plate. Oh, my mother was so embarrassed.

"I never was afraid for anyone to see me with my shoes off. I always walked alone. I never was lonely. I danced naked in the wilderness. We had a cabin in the mountains when I was small and I played with hornets, wasps, and birds. I danced naked in the wilderness, everything was my friend. But then one day my mother found me and told me I had sinned. I never did undress again and dance around. Until that day I never thought of what other people were going to think or say. I just grew like Topsy.

"When they put me under ether it was goodbye, I thought. 'I'm gone,' I said to myself, 'I'm going down headfirst into a dark pit.' So I wiggled my finger to stop them from burying me. I felt like a house, and they were putting in doors and windows, just banging away.

"When I was a child, people believed old women were witches.

Who Wrote the Book of Love?

They thought old women could turn themselves into cats, get into people's drawers, steal things. They believed this.

"I died on my grandfather's bed. Oops! I was just a baby then, he lost his foot in the Civil War. Tried to stop a rolling cannonball by sticking out his foot. I was wrapped up in a blanket on his bed when he finally died. I saw my grandmother die too, very calmly. 'Rest in peace' was her expectation. I have no fear of death. You may pick me up dead someday in the garden. I'm the last leaf on the family tree:

> " . . . if I should live to be
> The last leaf upon the tree . . .
> Let them smile, as I do now,
> At the old forsaken bough . . .

"If only we knew what the end of us was. Once I heard a voice, very steady and quiet. 'You are going to die,' it said. I didn't fight it. I was tired. It was like a realization."

Rose in her garden digging irrigation channels, passersby stopping to look or to ask for flowers, amazed at what she's made of the vacant lot. "I'm in hibernation now," she says, toes out, feet flat, cap on her head. "I walk alone. I told the children, 'Shoo, out of the nest.' I made a lot of mistakes. I don't think I'd have children again.

"My husband never meant that much to me. He was the same outside the family as inside, the same with everyone. He left me to care for things. My husband was a very popular man when we were young, an athlete, but three days after the wedding I rued it. I gave up my freedom, you see. 'After twenty-four, a girl no more.' You didn't divorce easily in those days. There were women and there were ladies. Ladies didn't divorce. There was another man who wanted to marry me, but he went into the Army and by the time he returned I was gone. After all these years he tracked me down. Called me up and said he still loved me, that he never had married. Wants to see me. On the phone he said: 'Is this Rose with the blue eyes and light brown hair?' 'Not any more,' I told him. I never felt that kind of romantic love.

No. I walked alone. I can't think of a thing on heaven or earth that could move me to remarry. My husband said that. 'You're a one-man woman,' he often told me. Patting himself on the back, I suppose.

"After my father died my mother married again. I set myself against her, told her not to. Do you know what she did? Just before the ceremony she switched me, three times in one day. I was a hard child.

"When I was at college, a professor wondered about me. 'Who is that girl who walks alone?' he asked. That was me. Now I walk alone. That fellow calls and wants to see me after all these years. Still loves me, he says. Well, it's too late.

"My grandmother was a fine woman. She was a tall person, from England, very beautiful. She lived by the Bible. When I was a child, I would put my head in her lap. 'Now, Rose,' she'd say, 'have you done anything wrong? Be sure to ask God for forgiveness or you'll be punished.' She never said what the punishment was. 'God is love, too,' she told me. Then grandmother would tuck me into bed, snug and safe. As soon as she was gone, I'd pull the covers over my head so God wouldn't be able to see me."

One day the man who had loved her so many years drove up from Oklahoma in his camper. He stayed only several hours. "I made another mistake," she said after he left. "When he came in, I was surprised at the way he looked. I remembered him from way back then. 'Why, you're an old man,' I said to him. I guess that put him off."

On her own, Rose struggles to orient herself. "Which door did I come in?" she asks to get her bearings, constantly having to backtrack to discover what she was doing. Events merge, jump out of sequence, confuse, intimidate. As she works in her garden one day, there's a gunfight across the street. A man threatens to kill his child; police shoot it out with him. Hearing the shots, Rose is certain the sounds are either in her inner ear or else happened years ago.

A week later she sees a monkey in a tree and calls the police. The monkey turns out to be a cat. And late one night she sees a man

Who Wrote the Book of Love?

feeding a raccoon right under her window. As she looks out into the darkness, the colors are phenomenally intense, her garden like a fairyland. She has no way to establish whether what she sees is real or not.

Thirty years ago, just out of the service, her son met a woman on the train and, within the day, asked her to marry him. Rose argued with her son, saying it was too precipitate, but to no avail. Years later her son's wife became epileptic. In a cruel trick of memory Rose now sees the two separate events as one. "Son," she has herself saying to him when they argued that day, "son, don't marry her. She's an epileptic." And what she remembers as her son's anguished reply keeps haunting her: "Mother, how could you say such a thing, how could you?" Her crime never having been committed—at least not in this form—there is no one to absolve her.

Each night Rose barricades the door. The cats take their places, one on the mantel, two by the heater, three on the bed. She drapes a black cloth over the songbirds' cage, and, suddenly, the din stops. Alone, adrift in the flow of the many people who have been part of her life, she reaches for something sure. Her grandmother. Wondering what will bloom in the morning, wondering if her sense of smell will return, struggling not to nod off involuntarily, she prays as she did as a child:

> Now I lay me down to sleep,
> I pray the Lord my soul to keep.
> And if I die before I wake,
> I pray the Lord my soul to take. Amen.

"I always add the Amen," Rose says.

 Just out of prison, dizzied by the flow of so much life around him, he calls from the station to tell her he's on his way. They've waited for this nearly two years. Two years, one thousand letters. His speak primarily of prison life, imparting its every specific not only to tell her just where he is, but also to suggest a corollary—that its qualities are becoming his.

For nearly his entire term her letters are full of love; almost to the very end she's unyielding in her affirmation. "And here I am," she writes, "hovering around your aura. Where before it was purple and red, thunder and lightning and extending two feet before you, now it is smaller. Now the outer edges are only just visible, the rest contained and multihued, the rim a dark but bright blue moving into pale yellow. And then, where no one can see, it deepens into a steady strong golden color, which in turn surrenders to a flaming center of red. Before, the energy frantic and realized. Now, the energy sure and potential." At no point does she believe that, world so diminished, his spirit is dying.

A few months before he's to be released, still presuming his strength, writing to the man he was, her letters change. So long has he been gone, so long has she waited, that she examines and reexamines the difficulties they've had, balancing this possibly compromised past against a putative future. Questions begin to fill her letters. What will it be like? Will you love me? What form will our love take? Will the future justify the time I've waited? Are you who I think you are? Though he sees what she's had to endure, though he knows he shouldn't have let her share his imprisonment, he makes no response to her questions. He hopes only to survive.

Out on the street he hurries to her house. Two years in prison

Who Wrote the Book of Love?

have left him, at this moment, only the absolute need to have a woman, any woman. Whatever else she may be, she is there, waiting. So much violence, so many penises, so much homosexuality, for him love has been reduced to sex, sex in turn reduced to rape. Coming from the very bottom of the bottom, then, he reaches her door.

He does not see the flowers, he does not see the sunlight pouring through the windows, he does not see her paintings on the easel, and, above all, he does not see her.

They embrace. He pulls her to the floor and enters her immediately, glad most of all not to be in *her* but to find that he has his manhood. Making no effort to meet her needs, he spends himself immediately and pulls away.

She stares at him, silent. Where to begin? And then, feeling something trickling down the small of her back, she touches her finger to the spot, bringing it around to examine. Blood. Startled, she turns to look at the floor where she lay beneath him. There she sees more blood, and some shreds of her skin.

 In my neighborhood we have mostly small two-story houses or four-room cottages with attics. The building code—encouraging a large tax base—allows construction to within a foot of the property line; walls of adjoining homes are often only two feet apart. Not for nothing are the bathroom windows frosted glass. Over the years owners eager for extra income converted garages to apartments or added small rental units. Most of these structures are freestanding, but on warm weekends the cumulative effect is of a tenement that's been flattened and spread. In a two-hundred-foot radius, for instance, there can be twenty barking dogs defending twenty separate yards.

Before he moved his family over the hills my landlord lived in this house. That was when he built a studio apartment against the back of the old tool shed which sits on the front of this eighth-of-an-acre lot. There's the street, the shed flush with the sidewalk at the forward edge of the property, the studio abutting the shed, a twelve-by-twenty-foot lawn, and this house. The walkway back to the house passes the rear wall of the studio. Garbage pails for both units sit near the studio's front door. All in all, it's tight.

When my new neighbor moved into the studio, he seemed to share my unspoken sentiment that in such circumstances good fences make good neighbors. In the absence of a fence we simply kept what distance we had; we were polite, but no more. Given the drummer next door, the handyman behind me, and the many dogs seeking *Lebensraum*, I appreciated my new neighbor's restraint.

He lived alone in the studio, and, it seemed, never had guests. His mailbox was always empty. Apparently he was divorced, his wife living somewhere in the area; every Saturday his young daughter appeared to spend the afternoon. My neighbor worked a regular week,

Who Wrote the Book of Love?

and soon after his return each evening I'd hear the TV go on. When the curtains were open, I could see a living room furnished only with a sofa, lamp, and two chess armies confronting each other on a card table.

Sometimes, for very good reason, one draws a line, but then later, forgetting the original impulse, one crosses it. This is what happened when, though still zealous of my privacy, I lingered on the sidewalk one afternoon as my neighbor approached the garage in a brand-new car. Our first conversation, taking place more than a year after he moved in, centered on why he replaced his old car, what options he ordered, the price, taxes, and insurance costs. Our exchange was simple enough, and I wondered if I hadn't been too rigid in keeping my distance.

About a week later I saw him pull up driving a taxi. As he backed in to the curb he smashed the fender of the parked car behind him, giving it a tremendous blow. Getting out of the cab, he walked back to survey the damage and saw me standing there. "Fuck it," he said with a thin laugh. He seemed exhausted.

At the moment I thought it might be the heat. We were having a drought, barely a drop the whole winter, and now, well into the normal dry season, there was no possibility of rain for another five months. Already the air was foul, the hills brown. Each sunny day—and every new day was sunny—promised only to burn us out.

Late that night, windows wide open, having trouble getting to sleep, I heard incredibly loud shouting coming from the studio apartment. "I'm strong!" my neighbor was bellowing. "No one can tell *me* what to do. I'm powerful. *You* can't tell me what to do. I'm powerful. Listen to me!" His voice kept breaking, as if he was in tears. After several endless minutes he stopped.

When we passed in the morning, he motioned me over.

"Sorry about last night," he said. "I guess I got a little out of hand. I was just setting some things straight with myself. My former wife's been giving me a hard time, boss has been on my back too. You know how it is." He smiled, but looked wretched. Wearing boots, denims, and a Levi jacket, he appeared not so much rough and ready as forlorn.

That evening just after sunset I heard thunder, and, going outside, saw great cracks of lightning, strange for summer here, the more improbable because there seemed to be no moisture in the air. But then suddenly it began to rain, a hard rain, steady strong straight-falling rain that quickly flooded and drowned the dry ground. As I stood outside, laughing to see the downpour, my phone rang. It was my neighbor calling from twenty-five feet away.

"Say, man," he said. "I hate to bother you, but if you have a minute would you mind coming over?"

"Want a beer?" he asked when I arrived. "Sorry to pull you out of your place," he said, opening the refrigerator, "but like I told you this morning, I've been working on some things, and wanted to explain to someone. It's related to what happened last night. This whole business with my ex-wife, for instance. She has to let me see the kid every week, but she doesn't make it easy. We argue about it a lot.

"Anyway," he continued, "I've been figuring some things out, all at once, and I'm right at the place where I can make some big changes. See that chess set? Well, most nights when I come home from work, I make myself something to eat, catch the news, and then play chess."

"By yourself?" I asked.

"That's right. What I do is smoke some dope and then play solitaire chess. It gets my mind going, helps me set things straight. The point is that I can feel my power now, and I'm ready to do things differently. And this is what I wanted to tell someone. These are the four changes I'm going to make. One: no more arguing with my ex-wife. Fuck her. It's just a bunch of bullshit, and I can rise above that. Two: no more cigarettes. They're just killing me anyway, which is what they want you to do to yourself. Who needs it? I can quit. The third thing: no more masturbation. That's just not a good trip to be on, especially since now I'm single. And number four: no more dope for a while. It's not bad in itself, at least not for most people, but I need to stop for a couple months, slow things down. And since I have

Who Wrote the Book of Love?

this power, since I have it right now, I'm going to do it all. And I called you over to sort of be a witness to it." He was grinning, clearly pleased.

"So," he went on, "that's all I needed. Thanks a lot for coming over. Sorry to bother you."

"Anything else I can do?" I asked.

"No, man, that's fine. Just wanted someone to see this happen."

I ran back across the lawn, barely getting wet. Suddenly exhausted, I went inside and fell right off to sleep.

The summer passed slowly, even that night's heavy rain doing little to relieve the drought. Ranchers were already slaughtering cattle because of lack of feed, and the paper predicted higher food prices starting soon. In town water controls were being imposed, and the smog was heavier than ever. All neighborhood noises seemed amplified by the dirty air. Tempers were short, nights hot enough to justify homicide.

I went up to the mountains for a month, widening my space, and spent the first day back diminishing myself to fit the scale of the neighborhood. That evening I heard my neighbor screaming at his ex-wife over the phone.

From time to time after that I'd see him in his taxi smoking a cigarette, or sitting at the card table in his living room, playing solitaire chess, pulling on a joint. Always, except for the weekly visit of his daughter, he was alone. As summer became fall, his cab was parked in front of the garage at midday ever more often; many times it was late afternoon before he headed out again. If work was his handhold on life just then, he was losing his grip.

Sometimes, seeing his TV switch on when he returned from work, or hearing his end of an argument with his former wife, I'd think that she and I were the only two people who knew he was there.

 They bump into each other on the corner by the pet shop. He's carrying ten pounds of Kitty Litter.
"Why hello," she says carefully. "Long time no see."
"How are you?" he replies.
"Pretty good."
"Glad to hear it."
"You've grown a beard."
"You noticed."
"Of course I noticed. Why did you grow it?"
"The better to hide behind."
She laughs. "That's unlikely. So you won't have to shave, probably. God knows you scratched my face enough times for me to qualify as an expert on that."
"Reproaching an old friend?" he asks.
"No, not really. I could have complained then," she says.
"You did."
"Not as much as I should have."
"Well," he says, "at least you admit we're not total strangers."
She gives a tight smile. "I admit we once knew each other."
"Do you think so?" he replies.
She looks ready to walk away, and he rues his words: he wants to keep her talking. It's been three years.
"I saw your folks at Christmas," he says.
"You did? I didn't know that."
"Your dad invited me over for dinner when I called to say hello. As always, they couldn't have been nicer, but he seemed pretty depressed."

Who Wrote the Book of Love?

"He is. When we talk on the phone he's always sardonic. Everything I say he turns into something else."

"Well, he's seen a lot, no?"

"Haven't we all?" she says.

"Apart from having to leave your homeland and start life in a new country, you mean?"

"Just forget it," she says, again looking around as if ready to go.

"How's your brother?" he asks quickly.

"Oh, he's fine I guess. Going to graduate school."

"It should be good for him," he says. "He'll be a good teacher."

"Maybe," she replies.

"You don't sound very enthusiastic about things."

"Things are o.k."

"How's your husband?"

"He has a show of his paintings coming up. He's got a lot riding on it, and is worried how it will come out. He feels if he doesn't make it now, he never will."

"Surely you tell him there'll be many more chances if this one doesn't work."

"No."

"Well, Jesus Christ, you should. Look how long it took your dad to make it with his music. And anyway, you if anyone should know that life changes, that it brings the unexpected."

"Reproaching an old friend?" she asks, smiling.

"Possibly."

"So what are you doing now?"

"Still running the bookstore, and building a new boat. Hoping to go cruising again soon."

"Sounds good."

"It is good. Things have been going well. Not so bad to get older. A little more sense to match the nonsense."

"Is that an accusation?" she asks.

"For someone I haven't seen in three years?"

"I remember you as capable of anything," she says sharply.

"No fair."
"All right." She laughs. "I'll give you another chance."
"Thanks."
"Well, here it is. Do you think I'm still beautiful?"
"Do you want an honest answer?"
"Now I'm not sure."
"Well," he says, "for what it's worth, I think you looked better then."
"Thanks for nothing."
"You asked."
"I should have known better. You always did have a sharp tongue."
"Like I said, you asked."
"You're right," she says. "I did. I wish I wasn't getting older. Youth is beauty for a woman."
"You really think so?" he asks.
"I know so."
"Well, all I said was that you looked better *then.*"
"Meaning there's still hope?"
"Meaning you're still beautiful."
"That's nice of you," she says. "Even if it is out of character."
"Bad for good," he replies. "But I've seen you do worse. Nonetheless, I stand by my words."
"Well," she says, looking down the street, "is there any other damage we can do to each other?"
"Not much," he says, laughing, "at least not in a public place."
"You're not suggesting we go someplace else, are you?" she responds evenly.
"No," he answers, meeting her eyes, "I don't think I am."
"Then it's been good seeing you," she says briskly, extending her hand.
"I'll take a kiss for old times' sake," he says, "if you don't mind."
"I don't mind."
He watches her walk down the street, and then, turning toward

Who Wrote the Book of Love?

his car, notices that his arms are trembling. Still holding the Kitty Litter. When he reaches his car there's a parking ticket on the windshield.

At home, in the kitchen, he tells his lover about seeing his former wife.

"I still find it hard to believe," he says. "We could clearly still irritate each other, but mostly I was amazed that I didn't feel more. I kept thinking, 'We know each other, we could even hurt each other, but was I ever really with her, and for so long?' You know, if I met her at a party now, for the first time, I don't think I'd seek her out. And this is a person I once loved. Strange, no?"

She takes his hand. "I wish I had met you years ago."

"Before I met her?" he says, laughing.

"That's right."

"No, no, no," he replies. "Consider yourself lucky. I had a lot to learn."

"I do consider myself lucky," she says, smiling.

"Me too," he says, leaning across the table to kiss her.

They sit silent for several moments.

"Do you think it could ever be that way with us someday?" she asks, looking at him lovingly.

"No," he answers. "I don't think so. I hope not."

There he was, feeling out of place in paradise, almost as often as his friends told him the island was Eden. "No traffic jams, no smog, no hassles," they'd say, cataloguing the negative virtues. And they didn't have to labor what the eye could see—superb surf, remote mountain streams, waterfalls, rich soil. No indigenous predators.

Whenever they used the word "Eden," however, he'd grow impatient. At the least, surely there were other kinds of beauty, didn't they know? Hadn't they ever seen autumn's changes, or wakened to a crystalline morning after a heavy snow? Well, no, they hadn't, even if they had. From 2,500 miles across the Pacific they could see the mainland only through the wrong end of the memory's telescope, images reduced, lens cloudy. Traffic jams. Smog. Hassles.

Like other young white immigrants to the island, his friends did indeed have a bountiful life, tucked away in a shack against a ridge of mountains, raising ducks and chickens, picking the overwhelming abundance of banana, papaya, guava, and mango, spending long hours by the ocean. It was incredible to him how quickly the outside world faded beyond reach, trade winds soft on the cheek day after day, stars close each night, and, always, the amniotic waves. Much that elsewhere seemed quite ordinary and necessary here lost all meaning.

But it was also true, he saw, that the pleasure of relief could diminish to no more than the absence of pain. At one beach where they regularly gathered, the young whites manifested so little enthusiasm that their presence seemed to diminish the ocean, reducing it to no more than a bigger and better swimming pool. Perhaps, he thought, no physical environment alone sustained life: people re-

Who Wrote the Book of Love?

quired, and created, a culture, some culture, if only from the remnants of one they had repudiated.

Close as they were to the magic of the island's natural forces, the young whites seemed to him to refuse to acknowledge what was also special to the island, its human history and their place in it. Beyond sentimental images of the native past, for example, few of them were aware of the traditions of war and human sacrifice. Nor did they know of the decimation by disease of the island population after the whites came, or of the long struggle by imported laborers to win basic freedoms. But most of all they failed to understand that here they represented something beyond themselves as individuals. Here, where whites had conquered, where Chinese, Japanese, and Filipinos had worked—and still worked—the cane and pineapple, here they were, willy-nilly, whites. Haoles.

"That's the past," his friends often told him. "You're holding yourself back. This is what's real, right here, now. You should accept what's before you." It was, in so many ways, sound counsel. What more did he want? But always—even after the curl of yet another wave—he saw resonances of the island's past and future, felt sure that his tranquil friends paid a price for denying what was also true.

He saw it even in the haoles' sex. Given their lack of ties to the community around them, their good health, and easy near-nakedness, one might have expected that sex would be a primary focus of their lives. But, strangely, it was not. Often, lying in the sun after surfing, on the verge of a sun-blasted dream, he tried to explain it to himself. Perhaps, he thought, sex was too energetic for strangers to the tropics, too aggressive in so soft a land. Or perhaps mating required some special scent which the sun bleached out, the water washed away. Or perhaps the cost of being newcomers to Eden was to feel compelled to emulate its purity. The young haoles, he thought, had replaced physical love with religion and narcissism.

Once, a haole woman he was attracted to offered him her guru's latest technique. "Look into my left eye," she said, fixing on his. "Now say 'You love me.' " He did as she asked: "You love me." Words spoken, however, he felt that she in no way loved him more. That, even if she did, he liked her less. She was a fine dancer, brought him to the edge of joy with her Tai Chi, but there was nothing in her not capable of being reworked in the image of some new master by morning. And those haole women not lost in the ozone of religious search generally obsessed themselves with themselves, endlessly discussing proper diet or the best sun cream, stolidly planning under which stars to have a child Welfare would support for the next fifteen years.

Time passing, he found himself without sexual desire for the haole women baking in the sun. Here in paradise, moving toward misogyny, he was becoming an unwilling celibate.

Reaching shore one day after some fine body surfing, glad to be alive for the miracle of such waves, feeling that if need be he could live without close human contact, he saw a young Filipino girl standing on the beach. She was an acquaintance of his friends, and, when she waved to him, he came over to say hello. After they exchanged a few words about the surf and where the lobster could be found, he headed home, leaving her dipping a young boy in the water.

Though they had said almost nothing, as he walked away he was still startled by how enthusiastic she seemed. With the most casual phrases she'd suggested an exuberance he had almost forgotten. This is what he had been holding out for, he told himself, incredibly relieved.

Several days later, having haunted the beach hoping to find her, he saw her at the water's edge, again dunking the boy in the waves.

"This is my youngest brother," she said, laughing, as he approached. "He's four."

They stood together for several minutes, silent, watching the child, until finally, feeling clumsy, he said, "I know this may seem funny, but would you like to join me for dinner sometime?"

"Let me think about it," she replied, smiling. "I'll be down here tomorrow. See you then?"

The next day they met and walked on down the beach, soon leaving the sunbathers behind.

Who Wrote the Book of Love?

"How old are you?" she suddenly asked him quite seriously, as if continuing an earlier conversation.

"Twenty-eight," he said, barely controlling a grin.

"Have you ever been married?"

"Not yet."

"Why?"

"Well," he said after thinking it over, "not being married represented a certain kind of freedom for me. I spent five years with one woman, and I think you could say we loved each other, but for us both, given what we came from, marriage didn't seem like a positive thing."

"And now you're apart."

"Yes. Like married people, we were capable of separating."

"Was that an unhappy experience?"

"Separating? Yes, it was. It was unhappy."

They kept walking, silent for several moments, surfers riding in toward them, trades strong. At last she said, "Do you know Jesus?"

"Not the way you do, probably," he answered, spirits plummeting.

"Well," she said, "let me tell you what He means to me. My folks come from the Philippines, and that's where I was born. But I went to school here, and of course everything was very different from what it had been for my parents. They're good people, but they couldn't help me live this new life. I got into drugs pretty heavily. I was confused and unhappy. My parents kept telling me that I wasn't myself, but I didn't know who I was supposed to be any more. And then I found Jesus. Things have been better for me ever since.

"So, after you asked me out yesterday, I talked with our minister. He said if you didn't know Jesus, he just didn't think much good would come of us spending time together. But he told me if I liked you I should invite you to our service. I do like you, and I hope you'll come."

That same night he entered their small chapel up on the mountain as they concluded a discussion of the Psalm of David. One of the congregation, an elderly Portuguese rancher, was saying that to the Lord all people are sheep, and that sometimes, to have us do the right thing, the shepherd has to break the sheep's legs.

When everyone had spoken, the pianist started "Just a Closer Walk with Thee," and the minister, in a truly joyful disposition, eyes closed, face lifted to heaven, began to talk in tongues, returning to English occasionally to murmur, "Thank you, Jesus, thank you, Jesus." As the hymn continued on and on, members of the congregation fell to their knees, raised their arms, and testified.

The service drawing to a close, he walked out to the ridge, the whole island laid out below, air rich with ginger. To the north, on the windward side, was a lovely parcel of land, gulch and plain, that his friends were urging him to buy. Since the native owners had no idea of its worth in a speculative land market, the price was very low indeed.

He was lost in his thoughts when she came out of the church and walked over to him, taking his hand. "What did you think?" she asked. It was clear she hoped he'd say he had felt the Spirit. If she perhaps perceived how far he was from sharing her faith, she seemed to want them to be able to be together, and asked no more than this formula from him to allow them to proceed. Surely it wasn't much to say, no more than a white lie. What was so important? He'd done far worse. And he was alone and lonely. They could have some good times as long as it lasted. All he had to do was say a few words.

But he dropped her hand, and, as he did so, almost laughed. Paradise was driving him crazy! Mosquitoes were on his mind, the mosquitoes white men had brought to the island more than a century before. Piqued by being denied some native women, several sailors had intentionally emptied water casks fouled with mosquito larvae into the streams. It happened that the island birds, isolated for thousands of years from the larger world, flourished without tucking their beaks under their wings or covering their bare legs when they slept. The mosquitoes soon killed them off.

Within a week, having said goodbye to her that night, not having

Who Wrote the Book of Love?

purchased the parcel of land, he was on his way—home—to the mainland. On the plane he sat next to an elderly island grandmother. "Where are you going, tu-tu?" he asked her. She thought for a moment, and then started laughing. "I'm going to live with my daughter and her family for a while, but that's all I can remember. I'm sorry, but I don't really know where that is."

Some minutes later she pulled at his arm. "Oh, I know," she said, very glad to have found the answer. "I know where I'm going. I'm going to the haole island."

There's Hank in the bathtub, a shank up on either rim, easing down from another day's carpentry and too many violent thoughts. Sitting on the toilet seat across from him, I'm ready to listen, if only for the possibility that words will stumble him safely to another side of the life he's been living.

"You know, man," Hank says, "I don't really mind all that much that Sue and I are separating. I can handle that. It's just that she's fucking every guy in town, starting with a list of my friends."

Good survival sense—fear of still another wound—keeps him from asking if she's reached my name yet. Though just after they parted, barely an hour after Hank called to ask me to do him a favor and "stay out of it," Sue came to my door. "I'm free now," she said, laughing, measuring my body with her eyes as if to see whether I'd fit. "Come by soon."

Hank shifts his weight in the tub, closes his eyes, groans with pleasure. "Isn't it true, Hank," I ask him, "that you spent time with other ladies while you lived with Sue?"

Memory cheers him. "This is fact," he says, grinning, "this is fact. Temptation—Maya, illusion—all too often manifested itself in the guise of loose women, leading me far from the Truth." He laughs. "It tormented me."

We're silent for several moments, mirror slowly fogging over. And then, hurt returning, he says: "You have to remember. I met Sue after my first marriage was shot. When Sue and I got together, I was going to school days, working in the mill nights, taking care of the baby the rest of the time. My first wife had taken off for God knows where. And never did return.

"Anyway," he continues, running some more hot water, overflow gurgling down the drain, "not only was I glad to meet Sue, but I guess you could say I had a lot of things I wanted to look into." He grins.

"But didn't Sue ever say anything about your seeing other women?" I ask him.

"Shit, yes," Hank replies vehemently. "She said I should do what I wanted. She said it didn't bother her. She said she didn't much care. That's what she said."

"And you believed her?"

"Hell, yes. You have to understand, I was almost ten years older than she was. She was coming out of that fucked-up family. She wanted me and she wanted things simple. And I made things simple. Christ, I was out there painting houses every day and she was tripping around or home having a good time. Making clothes, smoking dope, cooking, whatever. I don't begrudge her any of that, it was good for me too, but one thing's for sure: I gave her the shelter."

"But Hank," I say, "don't you ever think of it that Sue's just grown up now, that she's just getting some of her own, like you did? She was pretty young when you married."

Memory again gives him pleasure. "That is true, my friend," he says, smiling, "that is true. She was young and she was beautiful and she was just about untouched."

"So why not let it ride, why not cut her loose? You've had yours."

Hank sits up in the tub, staring at me. "I hear what you're saying, man. I say it to myself, too. Everything I'm feeling now goes right up against what I want to be, what I've worked to change in my life. I keep thinking about it. I know it's wrong, but I just can't help what I feel. What she's doing, it's tearing me apart."

 It was a slender thread, even as threads go, which he followed three thousand miles out to California. This is how it happened. Restless at nearly twenty-seven, a too predictable life stretching out before him, he quit his job as a draftsman, abandoning career prospects in the vague hope of becoming an artist. Leaving town, he came down to Boston the Summer of Love, the summer she happened to be back east on vacation visiting friends. And looking for someone to have an affair with. Seeing her in a laundromat with her infant son, he soon discovered that she was divorced and invited her out for ice cream. He had a sports car but was nearly broke. She had some money but no car. He found her attractive and as shy as he felt; she thought he was carefree and a rogue. They spent the next month traveling around New England, and had a pretty good time.

When she headed west, he said he'd be out soon, without making explicit whether it was California or her which attracted him more. Three months passed and still he didn't write or call, but her heart wasn't broken: she was busy with teaching and her child. She had no way of knowing he was en route the whole time, more or less. Back home liquidating his belongings; parents tearfully urging him not to be foolish; former employer offering him his job back; coming winter filling him with old fears. But then one evening as she finished preparing dinner he appeared at her door. Expressing no surprise, saying only "Hello, how've you been?," she handed him a plate of food, which, stumbling as he reached for it, he dropped. Exhausted from the days of driving, thinking what an entrance he had made, all he could do was laugh. She loved him for laughing.

He stayed in her apartment nearly a year, and for each it went without saying that he did so at least in part to save money. Getting

Who Wrote the Book of Love?

settled in his new life after a while, giving up the idea of being an artist, he did enough carpentry to earn the down payment on a ramshackle house near the Bay. It was a moment of change and possible commitment, which they almost wordlessly worked their way around by making her his tenant. She rented the front of the house for her son and herself; he took the back. The kitchen was hers. She prepared the meals, and, after some negotiation, he learned to do the shopping and wash the dishes. They split the food bill and made love in her sleeping loft, which he built.

Having tried it once, she had no use for marriage. As for him, still shaping a new life, cutting his teeth on the wide world, he didn't like to think of himself as being tied down. Landlord and tenant they were, then, and it suited them well enough, though they were as monogamous as any couple sworn to honor and obey.

After five years together they sought more distance from each other. A trip together to Europe only reinforced this desire: he spent the summer feeling that the austere romance of solitary wandering was being denied him, while she often thought of the men she might have been meeting. The trip wore them down, and it was all too easy to blame each other when they found themselves not so much travelers as tourists.

Back in California they agreed to part, after a fashion. That is, both continued to live in the house, but she had her lovers up front, while he built a separate entrance out the back. Even after he completed a kitchenette in his room, they still often ate together, and marked their changed relationship primarily by being more scrupulous about itemizing food expenses. Free of the burdens of intimacy, they were more polite to each other than they had been in several years.

Though her heart went out to an enchantingly impoverished young Talmudic scholar who finally left for the Holy Land owing her nearly a thousand dollars, after a while she had enough of romance. And her landlord/former lover, infatuation with a ballerina aside, logged enough hours sitting in bars sporting his new beard and pea jacket—lonely are the brave—to know what *that* life was like.

So once again they were alone together with her son in the house, but for a time simply as roommates and friends. Now less stifled by what they had created between them, life moving on, they were somewhat more gentle with each other. He no longer found it necessary to mock the affectations of her poet friends ("faggots," he'd once called them as he went out back to repair the septic tank); she got on him less often for drinking beer and watching sports on TV. Her son was old enough to shoot baskets with him, and he valued that. The house, which he never stopped improving, was steadily more comfortable, and they seemed, finally, friendly adversaries, a kind of family, which suited her. They spent many slow evenings together, preparing good dinners and entertaining company, without feeling the need to make each other over or deny each other any possibility. Things were o.k. for the moment, and who could pretend to know what would come next? They could have been sleeping together but weren't. As he said, she snored.

That summer a friend lent them a cabin in the mountains. They explored the area, climbed, swam, fished, camped out, chopped wood, watched the stars. For years strangers to small intimacies, they found themselves sometimes walking hand in hand or arm in arm, even occasionally kissing each other good morning. And they began to make love again.

For a time he thought she was putting on weight. Since she had always been trim, this surprised him, and of course in the mountains they were exercising heavily. He teased her about it, told her she must be getting older, but she simply smiled at him. One day, just before they were to return home, thinking it a foolish question and as always loath to play the fool, he asked her if she was pregnant. "I think I'm going to have it," was all she said, laughing.

When they came back to the city, he began converting the basement into a nursery, putting in paneling and insulation, laying a floor over the concrete foundation, drawing designs for a crib. As months passed and her stomach swelled he weighed names for the child. She

Who Wrote the Book of Love?

wanted a boy, he wanted a girl. "Someone not like me," he said. She did exercises and watched her diet; he continued his carpentry, shooting baskets with her son after work. And up in her sleeping loft late one night before he headed back to his room, as she murmured that the baby was kicking too hard, he—surprising them both—told her he loved her.

 They argue bitterly about their son's bad grades, each blaming the other, and then, still full of bile, retire to separate beds. After much tossing and turning, both begin to dream.

She sees them in the kitchen, bickering about household expenses until, too sick of it to hear another word, she takes up the meat knife and stabs him in the heart.

He sees them in the bedroom, where, again catching her lover's scent in the bedclothes, he shuts his ears to her denials once and for all and shoots her dead.

Grinning, they sleep.

Toward the end of the third year they lived together, her birthday several days off, he decided to arrange a surprise party. Calling their friends while she was at dance class, he then launched a series of obfuscations to cover his maneuvers. He "went down to the library" to see about having some chocolate pies made; "was out playing basketball" when in fact he was shopping for liquor, ice, and candles as well as rummaging through antique stores for a gift.

The day before her birthday one of the couples he had invited came by to give her a present. Since he'd been afraid she might wonder why friends weren't making much of her birthday, this early gift suited his purposes perfectly. Thinking it over, trying to make certain she suspected nothing, he gave her his own present that same afternoon, as if the actual day was of course less important than the occasion.

To be sure she'd be home and ready for company the next night, he mentioned casually that one of his old friends was coming into town and wanted to meet them for dinner that evening. It wasn't something they had to do, he told her, and of course if she had other plans she should say so. But if it seemed all right, his friend would pick them up around nine.

The next morning her parents called long distance, as did her sister. Several cards arrived in the mail. Though everything was proceeding according to plan, he grew more anxious as the hours passed, hoping no one would make a slip. When she expressed surprise that several of her closest friends had yet to call, he went out to "get some gas" and came back with a dozen red roses.

In midafternoon he had a bad moment: he suddenly remembered

that he was supposed to pick up the chocolate pies by two o'clock, but already it was nearly three. What if the bakery phoned?

"I'm off to get my laundry," he called out as he hurried toward the front door, cursing himself.

"Hold on," she said. "I'll come too. I can run in so you don't have to park."

"That's o.k. Why bother? I'll take care of it. But thanks anyway."

"I don't mind, really. Besides, I need some air."

"Well, I'm already out the damn door. Are you all set?"

"Give me a second. I'll be right there."

"Just forget it, will you?" he shouted, "I don't feel like waiting," and rushed out to the car.

"Are the pies done?" he asked the clerk behind the counter when he came running into the bakery.

"They certainly are," she replied curtly. "You know, you inconvenienced us. I told you we close early these days. We were just about to call you."

"But you didn't, did you?" he said.

"No. But we were going to."

"Glad I saved you the dime. Very glad."

When he came home, he had to drive around the block several times: he couldn't get to the garage to hide the pies until she finished watering the garden.

"Why were you in such a big hurry that you couldn't wait a minute?" she asked him as soon as he walked in the door. "And where's the laundry?"

"The laundry?" he said foolishly, having completely forgotten his pretext for going out. "Oh, well, you weren't ready. You know how much I hate to wait for you."

"But what about the laundry?"

"I was too early," he said, smiling in what he hoped was a winning way. "It wasn't ready yet. I forgot what time they told me to pick it up."

Who Wrote the Book of Love?

He was pleased with the lie. Criminals always use an alias with their real initials, he remembered reading. His fabrication was based on hard fact. Safe ground.

"Typical," she said, interrupting his self-congratulation. When are you ever going to learn? All that hurry, no time to wait for me, and for what? Nothing, that's what."

He was about to respond sharply, but caught himself just in time. Smarting from her cirticism, however, a little weary of all the dissembling, he had to console himself by anticipating how remorseful she'd be.

He had asked everyone to arrive just at nine. As the hour came and went he wondered if his watch was right, and began to regret that he hadn't chosen a place where the guests could all rendezvous. At ten long minutes after nine the doorbell finally rang. It was one of the guests, who, walking into the empty living room with a large shopping bag obviously containing a present, looked around and flashed a glance at him as if to say "Where the hell is everybody?"

"Hi," she said, coming out of the bedroom. "What brings you by? We're just heading out for dinner."

"You are?" their friend said, affecting surprise. "Well, I was just in the neighborhood and thought I'd drop in. No big deal."

"Want something to drink?" she asked.

"Sure, sure, that would be fine. Just a beer, thanks."

As she went to the kitchen, he quickly dropped his coat over the shopping bag. Just then the doorbell rang again. Two more friends, but only two. Realizing immediately that they too had come before the others, they hurriedly pocketed their gifts and stood smiling nervously as she came out to see who it was.

"I don't believe it," she said, laughing, apparently still unsuspecting. "This is incredible. We're just on our way out to dinner. If you haven't eaten, maybe you can join us."

And then the doorbell rang once more. This time, to his great relief, all the other guests came pouring in.

It was a fine party. After the presents were opened he went out to the garage and brought in the pies and liquor. People talked and danced for hours, and it was well after one when the last of their friends went home.

Turning the music off, he walked around the house picking up dishes and glasses, stacked them in the kitchen sink, and started washing. She came over and gave him a hug.

"Was it good?" he asked, turning to kiss her.

"Was it ever. Just wonderful. And I think everyone had a fine time."

"Me too. But suddenly I'm exhausted. Haven't played host for a while, I guess. And I have a headache."

"I'm done in too," she said, "but it was a lovely party."

Later, as they lay in bed, she asked him how he had managed to get everything taken care of without arousing her suspicion.

"Remember when I went to the library, played basketball, rushed out for my laundry?"

"Oh," she said. "It did seem a little weird, all of that, but you were so gruff I just left you alone."

"That was my secret strategy. I figured if I was an asshole you'd think everything was normal."

"Your words, not mine," she said, laughing, and kissed him.

"Well," he said, "I almost blew it with the baker by not picking up the pies on time, but it was much easier, all in all, than I thought it would be. You just aren't very hard to deceive."

"Yes I am."

"No, really, you aren't. You didn't suspect a thing."

"That's only because we never make a big deal out of birthdays. Do we."

"True enough, but even so you were amazingly easy to trick. I didn't even have to be a master of subterfuge, though on the other hand I think it was a great performance on my part."

"Don't be so pleased with yourself," she said, somewhat piqued.

"Hell," he said, smiling, "I'm just telling it like it is."

"If you want to know the truth," she retorted, "I've been humoring you all along. I figured it out from the very beginning."

"Bullshit."

"I did."

"Double bullshit."

"I mean it. I saw you coming in with the pies, through the kitchen window. And that's not all. I heard you on the phone, calling people. And anyway you were about as subtle as a Sherman tank. So don't be so smug."

"There's just no possibility you knew," he replied testily, half afraid that she had, but in any case totally unwilling to have his triumph compromised. "It's not so. You weren't at home, ever, when I spoke about the party on the phone, and you never saw me with the pies."

"Do I detect some doubt now in the genius?"

"Not a bit, damn it, not a bit."

"Well, I'm telling you I knew all the time. It was obvious. I just didn't want to deprive you of your little game."

"What crap," he said, losing his temper. "Hell, you were so gullible I could have been having an affair and you wouldn't have known the difference, that's how much you knew. I could have been having *two* affairs and you wouldn't have known."

"Yes I would," she replied angrily, "yes I would."

"No you wouldn't," he shot back, "no you wouldn't."

 From an early age Lisa zealously defended animals against human abuse and neglect, all through childhood imploring her parents to stop the car whenever she saw a stray dog or cat, the number of trips they made to the Animal Rescue League past counting, and, for her parents, believing. After an adolescence spent mostly on horseback she went out west to college, and, once there, promptly acquired two cats and a Russian wolfhound pup. She changed majors three times, severed and then restored ties with her family, was an acolyte and then apostate of several religious and political faiths, but always she loved her animals.

Wanting to travel when she completed her studies, she first drove her menagerie back across country. In no time at all her parents thought of the wolfhound as their own. Though loath to actually part with him, Lisa finally agreed, not only because her parents had an enormous yard where the dog could run free, but also because she planned eventually to return to northern California, and wasn't easy with the idea of the wolfhound living in a quake zone.

Her parents kept the dog, then, and cared for her cats while she wandered, but pressed her from time to time to reclaim them, especially when the wonderful male died shortly after a single kitten was born. Still not permanently settled and therefore reluctant to put the cats through any extra dislocation, Lisa nevertheless brought the mother and young daughter west by train, walking time and again down to the baggage car to give them more water or to soothe them. They wailed for three thousand miles.

Before fetching them, however, she had taken in a stray ringtailed skew-jawed orange tomcat she discovered hanging around her cottage, worn and clearly homeless. Almost immediately Señor del

[111]

Who Wrote the Book of Love?

Maverick—Maverick, for short—became master of the house, demanding and receiving snacks between meals, sleeping on Lisa's pillow, calling out to be let into the bathroom to drink from the small pool in the plugged tub. Even for a tom Maverick was willful, showing no interest, for instance, in any container of water placed by his food dish in the kitchen, spurning even a glass bowl she filled with small rocks and a miniature porcelain trout to simulate a mountain pond.

Lisa's affection for the stray orange tom was the more intense given the absence of her other animals and recent death of her favorite. Hearing Maverick at war out in the dark, ascertaining by hiding in the bushes that he was outweighed by his major adversary, she'd carry him on her shoulder and charge—hissing, gums bared, the two of them—at the invader. Over and again she cleaned abscesses in Maverick's war wounds. Though he yowled as she probed and salved, he seemed actually to understand the necessity and the concern. He should have, in any case: she explained it to him at great length more than once.

Since Maverick had grown accustomed to such intensive care, it could perhaps have been predicted that he'd go wild with jealousy at the sight of the two exhausted females Lisa brought back from the train station. Possibly she had imagined that, though they were spayed, he'd claim them as his own and settle comfortably into the role of paterfamilias. Instead, he repeatedly drove them under the house, and even after they were closed in the bedroom he raged at the door. Lisa tried first extra attention, then punishment, but he was adamant. There could be no compromise, he seemed to be saying, as if he could only lose were the two intruders allowed to move in.

Maverick was right, of course, though he might have cut his losses by accepting the inevitable. Could he only have feigned indifference Lisa might have sought him out, even understood his sacrifice and loved him the more for it, but despite his formidable will he was no strategist in matters of the heart. In his own eyes the injured party, by attacking the weaker females he became the apparent aggressor, incurring Lisa's anger, realizing his worst fears. Hurt and full of reproach, he took to spending long hours outside, coming in only to eat before heading right out. Occasionally, finding it intolerable to discover one of the newcomers asleep in his soft chair in the living room, or knowing all too well that they'd received some treat—brewer's yeast or chicken livers—while he was away, he'd attack. But finally, morose, he seemed reconciled, an exile in his own kingdom.

Meanwhile the females were settling in. They had shared a great voyage together, they were united in being the objects of Maverick's anger, and of course—if either remembered it—they were mother and daughter, but as the new life became normal their interests diverged. Initially, Lisa favored the mother, Titania. Old, black, and savvy, three times a mother, now a widow, she had a wonderful way of jumping onto Lisa's lap, following not the shortest trajectory—the hypotenuse of the right triangle formed by destination, floor directly beneath it, and point of departure—but sailing up, around, and over in a rich arc that carried her well above Lisa's lap before, as if rediscovering gravity, she dropped straight down onto it, landing light as a feather and without a sound. Without a sound, that is, until she responded to being petted, her purr crackling like a two-cycle chain-saw engine running at idle.

Quickly appraising her new home, Titania had never for a moment feared she'd be driven out. All too experienced with the vagaries of human affection, she understood what Maverick could not, that he was only hurting himself by resisting a *fait accompli*. Indeed, she was quick to turn insight to advantage, not only calling out in real terror when he attacked, but screeching whenever he drew near, grinning with satisfaction more than once as Lisa came running to chastise him.

After several months of being first in Lisa's favor, however, Titania developed a urinary disorder. As part of the cure she had to stop eating kibble, for years her exclusive diet (barring an occasional bird or squirrel). To do without it was the feline equivalent of kicking heroin. Though Lisa lavished her with bountiful portions of chicken parts, Titania was tormented with withdrawal pains. More than once

Who Wrote the Book of Love?

she vaulted onto the kitchen counter—forbidden territory, as she well knew—to pry open the cupboard containing the sack of dry food still being fed to the other cats. Both because the kibble only made her condition worse and because in going after it she knocked over flour, sugar, and spices, she and Lisa were soon at odds.

This yearning for contraband kibble quickly transformed Titania's whole rhythm of movement: now, like a commando behind the lines, she darted from place to place. Increasingly devious as she and Lisa became adversaries, soon she also came to hate being picked up: what had once presaged affection was now no more than the prelude to medication. Shunning Lisa, she concealed herself on a shelf in the closet, sneaking out only when she thought the cottage was empty.

With Maverick full of reproach and Titania in hiding, Lisa turned her attention to Titania's daughter. Chamie, the virgin princess. Spayed before ever even being wooed, Chamie was an enormous cat with beautiful tortoiseshell coloring, awesomely large paws, and four-inch whiskers to guide her bulk through narrow openings. Her true distinguishing characteristic, however, was shyness: she ran whenever she spotted human feet and legs approaching her; stayed under the house for hours if Maverick came her way; tucked herself far back under Lisa's bed each night. Time passing, however, the other cats keeping their distance, she noticed that Lisa now slept alone. So it was that Lisa woke one morning to find Chamie in the crook of her arm, dead to the world in full fetal curl.

Focusing her interest on this unbelievably demure creature, Lisa could pet her only along the cheekbones, and then with only one hand at a time. If picked up, Chamie would immediately wrestle free, run several feet away, and lick herself as if checking for wounds. Even when she slept, it was impossible to stroke her back or flanks. At first touch she'd open her eyes and solemnly regard the offending hand. If the violation didn't cease, she'd get up and leave.

Not the first human being to find reticence irresistible, Lisa began to ply Chamie with private snacks and late-night whispers of endearment. After several months of this, Chamie seemed to respond, sometimes holding her ground when humans passed, even running less when Maverick badgered her. Still swallowing his disappointment, Maverick could have told her how unfaithful human lovers can be, and of course Titania, the Billie Holiday of cats, could have sung Chamie some fine blues. But luxuriating in so much attention, just discovering love, Chamie wouldn't have listened. Occasionally now she let Lisa rub her chin, and of course such concessions only whetted the desire for more. Lisa laughed with elation when Chamie really purred for the first time, kissing her as the tiny rumble finally became audible.

One of the sets of human legs and feet Chamie still avoided belonged to the man who was courting Lisa, to that point without real success.

"Chamie's just playing hard to get," he'd say, watching Lisa give her caresses he feared he'd never receive. "The old 'not-until-we're-married' routine. But you'll tire of her as soon as you've won her, just wait and see." His words sounded as though Titania was his ghost-writer.

"You love animals more than you'll ever love me, I guess," he'd say, hoping Lisa would contradict him but drawing no response. "I should've been a horse. Then I might have a chance. But I should learn from the cats, shouldn't I. See how fickle you are. There's Maverick, poor rejected warrior. You once loved him best of all. And look at Titania over there in the closet. She has stories to tell, I can bet you that. Come on, big mama," he'd say to Titania as she gazed at him, pupils dilating, "come on, big mama. Help me out and tell it like it is."

Bachelor. An unmarried man. A man of marriageable age. "An eligible bachelor," for instance. Though the word has a musty feeling—"single" coming closer when matrimony is no longer the only point of reference—still it seems to fit John perfectly. He doesn't "live with someone"; isn't a "swinger." For all the freedoms at hand, there's a slightly out-of-date reserve in him that suggests older definitions: "a confirmed bachelor," perhaps.

After years of wandering as a free-lance photographer, John's returned to the small New Hampshire town he grew up in, caretaking some rental properties, living free in one of the apartments, auditing a few courses at the local college, working a large garden in the summer, seeing his small circle of friends, most of whom he's known since childhood. For pleasure and for extra income he repairs VWs and Porsches. A precise man of nearly thirty-five, he takes pride in his work, hates to be hurried, respects and accumulates tools, savors a Heineken dark at day's end, loves to give just the right gift, wears a fine Rolex on his left wrist, chooses his words carefully. "How to describe it . . .," he often begins after a long pause when someone asks him a question.

People in town remember John as a boy, like him well enough, are glad he came back after so many years away. Aware of and long since affected by modern sexual conventions, still they retain enough traditional categories to think of John as "living alone" and to leave it at that. Few people in town know he was once engaged to be married.

He'd been traveling in Europe nearly ten months that trip, catching photographic assignments here and there. Whaling dories in the Azores; wild horses in the Camargue; student demonstrators in Paris;

Basque shepherds in Spain. As Christmas approached he reached Copenhagen, and shortly after his arrival looked up the sister of a Danish journalist he'd once worked with in Amsterdam.

At first he couldn't tell whether it was Ingrid or her environment which attracted him more. She lived in a small village with her elderly parents; her people had been there four hundred years. Exhausted with travel, he was quickly overwhelmed by the extraordinary stability of the household. Snug under a down quilt as the east wind howled in from Siberia across Finland, he woke each morning to thank whatever gods were listening for showing him such peace.

Ingrid too seemed extraordinary. Tall, thin, very reserved, only just twenty-one, she had a fierce moral sense and need for commitment: she was only back in the village on holiday, soon to return to Africa where she was doing relief work with the Red Cross.

It was already a bitter winter, and as the days passed John and Ingrid took long walks while he shot pictures of the countryside. They looked out across the frozen Sound to Sweden, skated, skied cross-country, came back to the house for pork rib roast and rice pudding, cheese and herring, good Danish beer or some schnapps. When they'd move to the living room after a meal, Ingrid's parents smiling at him from their overstuffed chairs, bright floral designs of the Bornholmer clock just behind them like a garden out of season, Ingrid would translate as her father complained about taxes, or as John described his work.

"Do you like being so far from home?" her mother asked him.

"How to describe it . . .," he said. "You get used to it. I've been away much of the last five years. I have no more family there. Even the States now seems foreign to me when I return. But I like my craft, and this is one way to earn a living at it. Nonetheless, the traveling can wear you down. Sometimes I feel like an explorer; sometimes like a tourist; sometimes like a wanderer. It depends on the day, I suppose."

"Don't you sometimes feel like an artist?" Ingrid asked.

"I should have said that. Of course. That's why I take photo-

Who Wrote the Book of Love?

graphs. But just now I'm a little world-weary."

"*Traet af det hele?*" Ingrid's mother exclaimed. "*Det er en skam!*"

"Mother says what a shame that is," Ingrid translated, "to feel tired of life."

"Perhaps my phrase was too strong. What should I say . . . ? Simply that I've seen too many places."

"Then you should settle down," Ingrid replied firmly. "Make a home for yourself."

"Advice like that from you, Ingrid, when you're living in a foreign land?"

"Oh, I'm much younger than you are, John," Ingrid said, laughing. "Don't worry about me. I'll settle down someday, when I meet the right man."

Two weeks after he arrived, as they lit the candles on the Christmas tree, never even having embraced her, he asked Ingrid to marry him. When she nodded her head, smiling, he took her arm and crossed the room to ask her parents' permission.

Though they considered marrying immediately, Ingrid was set on returning to her work in Africa, while John looked forward to going back to the States and finding a place to settle down. She thought she'd feel as though she had done enough in Africa with one more year, and was eager after that to see America, even to live there if that's what he wanted. They could at least try it. He said the year would give him plenty of time to make a home ready for her. They agreed they wanted to live in the country.

Going up to Copenhagen for a week, before they made love she told him he was the first man she'd been with.

"I thought all Scandinavians were promiscuous," he teased her.

"The Swedes," she replied, laughing, "it's the Swedes."

When they woke the next morning, sunshine pouring through the frost-rimmed windows, she asked him if they'd be together as long as they lived.

"Do you want ownership or a lease?" he said, laughing.

[118]

"Oh, you mean man!" she cried, pushing him over, straddling him, putting her hands on his shoulders to keep him down. "Now you tell me."

"Tell you what?" he said, still laughing.

"Tell me," she said, pulling his hair. She was laughing too, but he saw tears in her eyes.

"All right, all right. I want you, Ingrid Pedersen, and only you. For as long as we live."

"You mean it, you horrible man?"

"I swear it, I swear it, but let go of my hair."

"You won't forget your promise?," tears still in her eyes.

"No, Ingrid Pedersen, I won't. I won't forget."

Friends in Virginia had often offered to let him build a house on their land, so he went there as soon as he returned to the States. Soon there were piles of lumber, sacks of cement, and a small mountain of shingles ready to use as soon as the rain stopped. He had also ordered bee colonies, thinking he could sell honey for a living if necessary. In addition he cleared ground for a garden. As he planned the house he'd think of Ingrid's home in Denmark. He couldn't offer her something with that kind of repose, but he'd build something she could make her own. Something they could make their own.

Two months passed quickly, and the weather was just clearing when his friends wrote him that they had suffered a financial loss and would have to sell the farm. They offered to let him buy them out, but he had no way to come up with the money and they needed cash. Depressed, he packed up his gear—yet another time, he thought—and moved down the road to a cottage he could rent. It wasn't at all the same, of course, particularly since the house he was to have built would have been his for life, but at the moment he was glad to find anything. He just wanted his life in order before Ingrid joined him. Already now three months were gone.

The cottage sat just behind a large farmhouse belonging to a couple with a child. As John moved in, washing windows, painting, scrubbing, refinishing the floors, he often heard the couple arguing.

Who Wrote the Book of Love?

As if to get out of the way, their five-year-old daughter would come back to visit, watching him clean, helping him plant his vegetables. Weeks passing, the girl's mother, Helen, sometimes visited too. As they got to know each other, they spoke about their lives, and one day she said she had just asked her husband to leave.

"Christ, we haven't been getting along together, that's for sure. I couldn't see the point any more. Life's too damn short. People don't have to do that to each other. I should never have married him, just lived with him without that extra expectation. It puts too much weight on everything. I don't mean, John, that you shouldn't try it with Ingrid if that's what you want. Everybody's different. But for me one good day is a pleasure, two something like a surprise. I'll settle for that from now on."

Though she couldn't have been less like Ingrid, John liked her a lot. Short, dark, almost plump, without any apparent concern for the world beyond her immediate circle, she loved to make sprout and seed salads, to search for mushrooms, to milk her goats. Soon she was bringing him gifts. A blackberry pie, some cream, a vest. She read his palm one day and told him he'd soon find love. "What kind of prediction is that?" he said, laughing. "You know very well that Ingrid will be here soon."

By now she'd been in Africa seven months. They were still writing each other several times a week, and he was pleased to see everything begin to fall into place. He had a lead on some land he could afford, and meanwhile the garden and beehives were flourishing. He was also busy restoring a wrecked Porsche he hoped to have ready for Ingrid's arrival. Though he was sometimes lonely, the countryside was beautiful, and most of what he was doing was for the two of them. Finally getting a darkroom set up, he developed the film from his weeks in Denmark. Soon images of Ingrid, her parents, her home, and her town were hanging on clothespins from wires strung in the living room. He pored over the contact sheets with an optical lens, trying to decide which shots to frame.

One warm night he and Helen were up late talking, frogs croaking over in the pond, sky teeming with stars.

"You know, John," she said, "I don't like everything about you."

"For instance," he said.

"Well, you're too intense sometimes, too correct. That's your uptight Virgo perfectionist speaking in you."

"Some people like me," he said, laughing.

"I like you too. Just not everything about you. But you'll do."

"Do for what?" He smiled.

"For me. For now. Don't worry. I've had two husbands and more lovers than I care to remember. We're just friends, that's all. So, here we are, together, it's nineteen hundred and seventy-two and a warm night. Do I have to explain it to you?"

"I guess not," he replied slowly, "I guess not."

The lovemaking was good, she lived right there, they enjoyed each other's company, neither demanded anything of the other, so they continued to sleep together. Occasionally Helen's husband would return to rage at her, but otherwise the next three months passed quietly. John continued to write to Ingrid, even arranged a phone call with her once. He said nothing, of course, about Helen, but considered it no worse than a sin of omission. He'd made his commitment to Ingrid, still felt it as real. He assumed she'd be hurt if she knew he'd been with someone else, but, weighing it carefully, decided that by his code he had hurt no one. He was over thirty, he told himself, old enough to distinguish between love and like. And there was no good reason for Ingrid ever to know.

About a month before she was to arrive, almost ready to put the finishing touches on the Porsche, winter coming fast, John told Helen he thought they should stop sleeping together. He wanted some time to be alone, to focus on Ingrid. Helen asked for one more night together, and in the morning told him that, just so he'd know, she wanted to say she'd never hint to Ingrid that they'd been lovers. He was relieved to hear her words, though he expected as much from her: that's who she was. Briefly, when they started sleeping together, he considered moving again before Ingrid came, lest his having been with

[121]

Who Wrote the Book of Love?

Helen somehow become an issue. That, he thought, would be insane: he knew his priorities. But now, somewhat surprised, he realized how much he'd miss Helen. Without ever using the word, she had given him love.

Two weeks before Ingrid was to arrive, as he was out cording wood, Helen came back to the cottage, weeping. As he pieced together what she was saying, he learned that she had seen her husband in town that morning. Apparently, when she again said she had no interest in getting back together with him, he threatened first to kill her and then to kill John. John, he said, was the reason she had turned against him. Finally, waving a pistol, he had shot himself in the head.

The next weeks were a nightmare. Being questioned by the police; arranging the funeral; caring for Helen, who was in shock; babysitting her daughter. Though Helen asked nothing of him, he of course felt an obligation to her, the more so because her husband had blamed him for the separation. Helen needed him, that was clear, and he stayed with her until the morning Ingrid's flight was due.

Driving the hundred miles to the airport, John was exhausted and in turmoil. Nothing was going as planned. He hadn't wanted to leave Helen, felt she still needed him, nor was he in any way ready for Ingrid. It was crazy: he had spent months preparing for her, had planned space and time to clear his life completely for her even after he was with Helen, but now he was rushing pell-mell to make it on time to meet her plane. The Porsche said it all: upholstery still torn, exterior not yet polished. He hated this kind of chaos. It offended his sense of rhythm, offended his sense of responsibility. To Ingrid, to Helen, to himself.

Coming off the plane, Ingrid quickly sensed something was wrong when John told her they wouldn't be going right home, that they'd take a short vacation first. His hope was to let Helen recover before he returned. As they drove up into the mountains, he stopped several times to make phone calls. That night in the motel room Ingrid asked whom he was trying to reach.

"Something unpleasant has happened. I'd rather not tell you just now. Will you forgive me?"

"I'm sorry, John, but I've come so far and things are so strange that I think you better try."

"I don't want to lie to you, Ingrid, but I don't want to tell you the truth tonight. Can you wait a day or two?"

"I don't think so. I'm sorry."

"How to put it . . .," he probably began that night in the motel room. Should he have lied? Should he have expected her reaction? Questions, years later, he still asked himself. Whichever, tears started down her cheeks when he told her about sleeping with Helen. And when he described the death of Helen's husband she started sobbing. She cried that night and all the next day. Then she asked him to take her to the airport. Nothing he could say changed her mind.

When her plane disappeared on the eastern horizon, he drove the hundred miles back down to Helen's house and found a note from her on the door.

"We're going out to California to see my folks. We have to get out of here for a while. Too much has happened. Thanks for everything. You've been a good friend. Take care."

Packing up his gear, putting it in storage, giving a neighbor the beehives, telling him to take the brussels sprouts and pumpkins from the garden, John got in the Porsche, and, nowhere else to go, headed back to the New Hampshire town he grew up in.

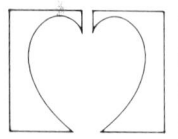 "So all in all," he's saying, "I think it's a good thing she didn't come. She really doesn't have any use for this kind of frenetic traveling, and of course at thirty-five I don't need to feel guilty about my style of doing things. Seeing her get exhausted and thinking it's a crazy pace. Which it is. Besides, we've barely been apart for four years. Good to separate for two weeks, just to be a little less taken for granted." This is a husband far from home talking with old friends, and, words just out of his mouth, a husband already ruing his suggestion that he and his wife need some time away from each other. An unfair dig at her, he thinks, so many thousands of miles away. Not really true, petty, pointlessly disloyal.

His trip is in fact incredibly hectic, and, though sure before leaving that he wouldn't think much about his wife, he often stops between meetings and friends to try to picture what she's doing at a given moment, careful always to allow for the difference in time zones. He sees her lying in bed, morning sun brightening the room, three cats for a blanket; bicycling off to dance class, closing the gate behind her; mixing grains for breakfast cereal. "She should have come," he sometimes thinks, seeing a street entertainer, an interesting bookstore, a good friend. "She would have liked this."

On the other hand, he has much to do, and there was in fact something arbitrary about taking the trip when he did, not to mention making it at all. At the least there was probably a better time, but he simply thought he wanted to go then, and committed himself. Though, as the time of departure approached, flying so far so fast seemed gratuitously violent, senseless, unnecessary. The morning he was to leave he and his wife sat out in the garden, cats chasing butterflies, birds at the feeder, squirrels scolding. Why go? But it was too late. "I suppose it's just as well she didn't come," he says to himself, more than once.

Throughout the trip he has the sensation that traveling itself makes him unfaithful to his wife. Not because he left her behind, or because he's free of the domestic burdens they normally share. But because, out of his own environment, changing with each city and setting if only to adjust to what is there held to be real, he feels uncentered, unaccountable, not himself. In that sense, inconstant.

As he promised, he calls her often, and she seems eager to hear him say that the trip will be shorter than the two weeks he had planned. But he tells her he's running hard and will barely return on schedule, feeling a touch of pique when she fails to applaud his efforts or to understand how much he's giving up—a trip to the country home of old friends, for one thing—to maintain his pace.

Lying in a hotel room one night, he dreams that all planes, cars, and trains have disappeared, that he must work his way overland on foot to get back to her. But there's some kind of war going on, he has to be careful. Towns burn; people are captured and killed. Lost and ill in his dream, he meets an old woman who gives him flower remedies: Pine, for those who blame themselves; Sweet Chestnut, for those suffering great anguish; Willow, for those who deny they deserved such adversity. And Holly, for those with no real cause for their unhappiness. "You'll find a home, never fear," the old woman tells him. "Some home. Does it really matter which?" In his dream he's ill for a very long time: at the moment before he wakes in the hotel bed, damp with sweat, he still has many miles to go.

Getting much business successfully accomplished the rest of his trip, he's ever more pressed and fatigued, but, the end in sight, he begins with relief to feel that of course it's the trip which is temporary, home of course which is permanent. The night before he's to return he calls his wife, trying several times but getting no answer. When, very late, he finally reaches her, she tells him she was out with a mutual friend.

"Where did you go?" he asks.

Who Wrote the Book of Love?

"To the movies."

"He just happened to call you?"

"He called and wondered if I wanted to go."

"Just like that? He never called to ask you when I was there."

"Of course not. He likes me, as you know, and thought I might be lonely with you away."

"That's consideration for you," he says sharply.

"Are you saying you don't think I should have gone?"

"No," he replies, suddenly exhausted, exhausted with himself, "no, I don't think you shouldn't have gone. What am I talking about."

"Still love me?" she says, laughing.

"Yes, dammit, I still love you, but we're very far apart. Too far apart. Time to get back together, don't you agree?"

"I agree," she says. "Why don't you be sensible and come home?"

Just before he boards the plane, he sends her a card. Though he's mailed one each day during his trip, all have been notes. Seeing and feeling so much, shifting inner and outer ground so many times, he's been unable to find a point of purchase on all the changes, settling for doing what he could—saying hello. But writing this card, now a man returning to his wife, he has his voice:

"I thought I'd forget you while I was away, not having, as you know, much of a memory. And, as you also know, believing myself unwilling to live any life except the one right before my eyes. But I want to tell you that to my great surprise, over all these miles, I've seen you all the time. I hope you're still there."

On the plane he sits next to some newlyweds. "Going on our honeymoon," the bride tells him. "And you?"

"Oh," he replies, "I'm going home."

"How long have you been gone?"

"Two weeks today."

"Two weeks can be a long time, particularly if you have family. I'll bet you're glad to be getting back."

"Yes I am," he answers, "yes I am."

Hours pass. He watches the last range of mountains finally give way to the coastal plain, the seat-belt sign comes on, and they prepare to land.

His wife is at the airport to meet him. Extremely pleased to see each other, they embrace, get his bags, and drive home. Once there, all he so recently only imagined quickly paints itself in. The plants, the rugs, his books, the bed, a quilt, the cats. When they make love, far from feeling strange to him after his absence, his wife seems only more herself than he remembered.

Waking in the middle of the night, he walks restlessly around the house checking the doors. Seeing his wife in the bed, hair spread wide over the pillow, chin as always tilting up and away, he thinks, smiling to himself, that of course he who returns has never really left.